DEDICATION

To my family - for your love and support, on and off the page.
And to my firehouse brothers and sisters, the ones who chase the flames,
the dreams, and the unknown.
Stay brave. Stay bold.

BADGE ON FIRE

Daniel Green

EXPLORERS EDGE PUBLISHING

CONTENTS

Prologue

The villa stood isolated against the dark sky, perched precariously on a cliffside overlooking the tumultuous sea below. Flames, spreading to every corner, blast-opened every glass window and decorated the veranda with warm hues of red, yellow, and orange. Like a disease unchecked, the fire consumed everything in its path, mirroring the uncontrollable turmoil within Jack's own mind. Heavy with stars, the night sky became a backdrop for plumes of thick, black smoke; the lack of nearby lights from homes or streets added even more drama to the fire, making it visible all the way down in Ensenada.

These flames were not a result of an accident or an act of God. A few yards away, on an overgrown hill that rose like a spine along the coast, Jack stood still in the shadows, watching the fire blazing, accompanied only by the sound of crickets and his troubled thoughts. A subtle glow came from his cigarette. His expression was calm, still, like the surface of a lake on a winter morning. It was only his eyes, reflecting the flames, which betrayed him with a storm of emotions. He nervously played with the zippo lighter in his right pocket, his fingers running over the J&J letters embossed onto the cold metal case. Jack & Jen. It was a special gift from his wife, a token from a better time, when the world made more sense, and the only flames he fought were the ones he knew how to put out, not start. He flipped the lighter open, letting a small flame dance for a moment before snapping it shut - thinking, this is the only part of Jen he still gets to have.

Before this blaze started, while the strong Mexican sun was setting, Jack saw a family enter the house - his planned target - Gustavo Calo, his wife, and a young boy no older than ten. "They aren't supposed to be here," Jack mumbled, expecting to catch Gustavo alone. It was too late now, and he wasn't supposed to be thinking about fixing this unexpected surprise. *What is done is done*, he reminded himself. That man had to die. Jack knew that much - Calo had uncovered plans about their operation and was preparing to strike back. His attack could compromise everything - and everyone - Jack had worked so hard to keep alive. Taking down the device that triggers the fire risks him getting exposed - and getting caught was a worse sentence than death.

Collateral damage, Jack thought bitterly, and then quickly realized this is exactly what his mentor, Xavier - a man of reason and logic rather than emotion, would say. *I guess it's true what they say: you slowly become more like the people you spend the most time with.*

The distant wail of sirens grew louder, pulling Jack away from his thoughts. "About time," he exclaimed. The famous Los Fuegos Crew arrived on the scene. He recognized their trucks, which screeched to a halt, and the brave local firefighters jumped out without wasting another second. Jack watched from the shadows as they moved quickly, rolling out hoses and shouting commands, and couldn't help but notice the irony. He was the one who donated most of the firefighting equipment they were using less than a day ago. Well, at least it's put to good use, Jack concluded. He recognized a young man with a funny mustache who had thanked him profusely for the gear, his face now beaming with a mix of pride and concentration. Now, that same brave fellow was battling a fire Jack was responsible for, risking his life, desperate to stop it from spreading further from the villa for the good of the wildlife and the nearby residents of this small Mexican town. Soon after, the police and ambulance cars arrived, too. There is no way anyone could have survived this, Jack thought, almost reassuring himself.

He turned away, unable to watch any longer, suppressing the thoughts of the young boy who got caught in his web of revenge. The flames crackled behind him as Jack walked away, his boots crunching softly against the dirt road. He didn't look back. The sound of shouting and the rushing water faded into the night as he disappeared into the dark, the lighter still heavy in his pocket.

Somewhere deep inside, a fire continued to burn.

PART 1: SMOKE AND MIRRORS

CHAPTER 1

The city of Berkeley was one of contrasts. Nestled against the backdrop of rolling hills and vibrant city streets, it was a perfect blend of innovation, activism, and an older, quieter life. It buzzed with youthful energy while also offering pockets of tranquillity in its sun-dappled public parks and quaint, tree-lined neighborhoods. When Jack Singer moved there years ago to attend the University of California, he didn't expect to stay as long as he did, much less to meet his wife Jen and start a family.

His initial plan was a simple one: graduate and then travel across Europe, maybe working as a surf instructor in the summer and a ski teacher in the winter months. His love for sports and adventure wasn't just a hobby but a lifeline—a way to escape the day-to-day stressors of life. Coming from a broken family, Jack had developed a desire to escape, and nature provided him with the peace he longed for, like nothing else ever could. But life doesn't always work according to plan, especially not in your early adulthood.

When Jack and Jen fell in love, it felt as though the rest of the world melted away. They spent countless evenings dreaming about their future, painting vivid pictures of the life they wanted to build together. Jen spoke with bright, eager eyes about starting a family and finding a cozy house nestled in one of Berkeley's quiet neighborhoods. She had grown up in the city, surrounded by lifelong friends and close-knit family, and couldn't imagine leaving it all behind.

For Jack, it was different. He had always imagined a life of adventure, travelling the world and chasing the unknown. But while listening to Jen's dreams about their future together, he discovered a part of himself he hadn't known existed—a part that yearned for roots, stability, and permanence. He wanted to build a life worth protecting, a home filled with love and laughter. For the first time, he felt a deep desire to provide—not just materially, but emotionally, to be the pillar Jen could lean on, to be the "hero" she often called him, to his amusement and disbelief. He wanted to live up to that title, not just for her, but for himself. Her unwavering belief in him stirred something inside, a quiet sense of purpose that began to overshadow his wanderlust.

When the opportunity to train as a firefighter presented itself, it felt like fate. The job called to his thrill-seeking nature—offering the adrenaline rush of the unknown—while also aligning perfectly with his newfound desire to protect and serve. He thought of Jen's smile every time he put on the uniform, knowing he was working to give her the life she dreamed of.

Over the years, Jack threw himself into his work with the same passion he had once reserved for his sports and travels. He wasn't just good at doing the job; he excelled. His natural instincts under pressure and his calm leadership earned him respect among his peers, and before long, he climbed the ranks to become Captain at the Berkeley Fire Department.

Through all his accomplishments, it was always Jen who grounded him. She was the reason he pushed harder, the reason he stayed in Berkeley instead of chasing distant horizons. Her belief in him became the compass he followed, and the family they built together became the anchor that held him steady.

As Jack embraced his role, both as a firefighter, a partner, and eventually a father, he found that protecting the city that held his heart became his greatest adventure yet.

***

The station where Jack was based sat at the edge of a bustling neighbourhood, a squat, utilitarian building with wide garage doors that gleamed in the sunlight. Surrounding the station was a vibrant tapestry of Berkeley itself: old brick buildings, interspersed with modern cafes and bustling shops. Locals—from curious children eager to explore the gleam of fire trucks, to families and business owners who sometimes dropped by with donations of meals—were drawn to its open doors. Behind those doors was camaraderie, laughter, and a sense of readiness. The crew wasn't just a group of colleagues—they were a family, bonded by the unpredictable rhythm of their work and the shared understanding that when the alarm rang, every second counted. Although diverse in background and personality, they shared a mutual respect and an unspoken commitment to the job, which was the glue that held them together. The team was split into three shifts - A, B and C who worked on a 48/96 work schedule: on-duty for 48 hours (2 days), then off for 96 hours (4 days). While there were a lot of perks to having so much time off, the schedule was strict and this meant some crew members would miss holidays, birthdays, and other important events.

The crew at Fire Station #5 was a colorful mix of personalities, each bringing their own quirks and charm to the firehouse. Bob Washington was the station's heart. In his mid-40s, with a stocky build and a kind smile, he had a natural ability to bring calm, even in the most chaotic situations. Bob wasn't just a firefighter—he was a mentor, a sounding board, and a source of quiet wisdom.

During the 48-hour shifts, his deep baritone voice could often be heard humming bluesy tunes or gently teasing one of the rookies while he tinkered with the trucks. "Tom, you're overthinking it again," he'd say with a knowing grin, watching the younger firefighter fumble with a tool. At home, Bob was a devoted husband and father to two teenage daughters, who were the stars of his stories around the firehouse. Whether it was their latest softball game or a family BBQ, Bob's anecdotes always brought a smile to the crew's faces. His love for his family was palpable, and it made him a grounding presence in the station—a reminder of why they all did what they did. While Bob was beloved by his team and the other shifts, his laid-back nature sometimes caused headaches for the meticulous crews on C shift, like Jack and Ria. "I swear, it's like a hurricane blew through here," Ria muttered once as she restocked a poorly organized medic kit. Jack gave a rare smirk. "That's just Bob's charm rubbing off on them."

Maria Gonzalez - or Ria, as she insisted everyone call her - was the station's fire medic, a petite yet fierce woman in her early 30s. Born and raised in East Oakland, she had a sharp wit and a no-nonsense attitude that commanded respect from the entire team. She was known for her ability to stay laser-focused during emergencies and her quick thinking, which often saved lives. When she wasn't riding the truck or restocking the medic kits, she would be keeping up with the boys' jokes and taking none of their nonsense. "Don't start something you can't finish, Abe," she'd quip during their banter, her eyes sparkling with amusement. Her personal life was a bit of a mystery that she didn't naturally talk about, but the crew knew she was close with her younger brother, whom she helped put through college.

Jack, a natural leader and the station's Captain, was also part of C shift and had earned a reputation for his precision and discipline. While B shift's easygoing nature often left things undone, Jack saw it as just another challenge. "Let's get this sorted," he'd say, more resigned than annoyed, as he reorganized hose beds or restocked supplies.

His dynamic with Ria made C shift tight-knit and efficient. They had an unspoken understanding, each anticipating the other's moves on the fire line. Ria once joked, "Between me keeping the boys in line and you fixing Bob's mess, we're basically babysitters." Jack had laughed, though the weight of his double life often kept his humor in check.

Abraham O'Neil was among the loudest of the bunch, his booming laugh often echoing through the halls. Born in Ireland, he was one of the young boys who made their dream of becoming a firefighter a reality and had been with the team for over a decade now. His family moved to Berkeley to start a new life, and he certainly met everyone's expectations. Abe was always a joy to share a shift with - his banter was as much a part of the team's mornings as the smell of coffee and the hum of the dispatch radio. That man had an exceptional talent for turning even the dullest task or darkest moment into a joke, and this certainly kept the team's spirits high, even on grueling days. Single and unapologetically so, Abraham often joked that his Labrador, Zain, was the only commitment he needed.

But his relationship with Jack's family ran deep. Abe had been an extended part of Jack's life, joining them for Thanksgiving dinners and helping out whenever Jen needed an extra hand or Ellie - Jack's daughter - needed babysitting. On their days off, Abe and Jack would often head out on adventures—surfing, kayaking, or climbing. Abe O'Neil also didn't miss the opportunity to grab a pint and chat about the football, which often balanced Jack's seriousness. Their bond was unshakable, built on years of shared experiences and unspoken trust.

O'Neil was in the middle of a good-natured argument with Jay, one of the rookies, about who was worse at making coffee. "This is not coffee," Abe would say to Jay. "This is a war crime!"

Jason "Jay" Patel was the newest member of the crew, and his youthful enthusiasm was as endearing as it was exhausting. At just 25, he was fresh out of the fire academy, armed with a degree in mechanical engineering and an eagerness to prove himself. Jay's technical skills were unmatched; he could fix almost anything, often leaving the older crew members scratching their heads in amazement. "Kid's a genius," Ria would say with a chuckle, "but he's got the common sense of a traffic cone."

The team teased him mercilessly, but it was always in good fun. Jay, for his part, took it all in stride, determined to earn their respect. His inexperience sometimes got the better of him, and he had a tendency to overthink things, but the crew was quick to guide him when he stumbled. Abraham, in particular, had taken Jay under his wing, and their dynamic was one of playful ribbing mixed with genuine mentorship. "Keep that helmet on straight, rookie," Abe would say, slapping him on the back after a call. Somehow Jay reminded him of his younger brother, and he loved working with the kid because he felt that feeling of being whole again.

Life at the firehouse followed a rhythm dictated by the 48-hour shifts. Mornings began with coffee and the Captain's briefing, where they'd discuss the previous shift's events and the day's agenda. Equipment checks were meticulous—hoses inspected, water tanks filled, and trucks cleaned until they gleamed. Between calls, the crew tackled everything from hydrant inspections to public outreach events. They took turns cooking meals, a task that often turned into a battle of egos. "My chili is undefeated," Abe would boast, only to have Ria roll her eyes. "Your chili is so spicy, it could set a fire to this place. You're lucky we know how to put one out."

Evenings were more relaxed, with games of basketball or Liars Dice filling the downtime—at least until the next 911 call came in. The unpredictability of the job meant they had to be ready for anything, and their bond was what made it work.

Despite the camaraderie, the 48-hour shifts took a toll. Sleep was often interrupted, and the emotional weight of their work lingered long after the fires were out. But in those rare quiet moments, when the station was still and the only sound was the hum of the trucks in the bay, they found solace in knowing they were in it together.

***

Abe's phone buzzed, interrupting their heated coffee argument.

"Speak of the devil," Abe muttered, grinning as he picked up. "Morning, Jack. You alive over there, or should I send a rescue team to drag you out of bed?"

Jack's voice on the other end was gruff. "I'm fine. What's up?"

"Nothing urgent," Abraham said, leaning back in his chair. "Just wanted to check if you're still good for that equipment run to Mexico next week.

Ria and I were going through all the stuff we wanted to donate and making inventory, but I wanted to double-check before I bothered with all of it. Oh, and you're on for the hydrant inspections today, right?"

There was a pause on the line before Jack replied. "Yeah. I'm on it. Thanks for checking in. I'll drive down there soon."

Abe frowned slightly as he hung up. Jack had been distant lately, and Abraham couldn't shake the feeling that something was off. Not to mention that the Captain was always punctual - he would always be the one greeting you when you entered the station, ready to step into his shift. He reminisced about the time when Jack used to be a lot more cheerful, more social, full of an unquenchable thirst for life and adventure... But before he could dwell on it, the dispatch radio crackled to life, pulling him back into the station's rhythm.

***

Jack struggled to wake up that morning, physically exhausted after the long drive home and mentally drained. He got out of bed, almost angry at himself - *what happened to the man he once was?* He used to love the discipline of being a firefighter, the early mornings, the sense of responsibility. Lately, even the act of getting out of bed felt monumental. Ever since Jen died, he has gradually been fading away, not realizing it. The nightmares hadn't helped. He hoped the water from the shower could wash away his dreams about the villa and put down the flames in his mind. Despite his exhaustion, he was a man of precision. He never left a sloppy scene behind himself; he always calculated everything to the smallest detail. Maybe that was his curse.

Jack made his way to the kitchen, putting on a brave and friendly face for his daughter, Ellie.

"Ellie, come on! I am making you your favorite breakfast today." - Jack shouted through the bright, open kitchen, hoping it would reach Ellie's bedroom and get her out of bed. He was making pancakes, hoping they would taste at least a little bit like Jen's. There was never a moment when he would make pancakes and not think of her. Even though it's been two years, there was rarely any moment he wouldn't think of her. He cursed his luck and kept trying to bargain with the past, wondering if things would have been different if he had gone to pick up Ellie from school that day. Ellie's footsteps helped Jack snap back to the present moment.

She shuffled into the kitchen, still in her pajamas, her hair a tangle of curls. At only thirteen, she had the same sharp, inquisitive look in her eyes that her mother used to have, the eyes of someone wiser than their age.

"Morning, kiddo," Jack said, forcing a smile as he set a plate of pancakes in front of her.

Ellie looked at him, her brow furrowed. "You okay, Dad? You look... tired."

"I'm fine, sweetie." Jack lied, pouring himself a cup of coffee. "Just a long week."

Ellie didn't look convinced, but she let it go. "Are you working all day?"

"Yeah," Jack said, sitting across from her. "But I'll be back in time for dinner. Aunt Meg said she'll pick you up from school."

"Okay." Ellie poked at her plate, her expression distant. Jack felt a pang of guilt. He knew he'd been absent lately, not just physically, but emotionally. He wanted to be better for her, but the weight of his double life made that harder every day, and he felt they were slowly drifting apart.

"Come on, kiddo, go and get dressed. I will drop you off at school before heading to the station."

Ellie stuffed a piece of pancake in her mouth and a few blueberries as she lifted her backpack. Jack grabbed his car keys and followed her out the door. The air was crisp with the promise of another sunny Berkeley day, and a pleasant taste of saltiness in the air coming from the not-so-distant ocean, inviting all the surfers out. Jack enjoyed taking the usual route to work - there was something about having a solid routine that helped bring him back to the present, pulling him away from his thoughts, if even for just a brief moment.

He drove past a cafe where he and Jen would grab breakfast early in their relationship. It was a small, seemingly unnoticeable diner with food saturated with fat and smiley staff topping up your hot drink regularly. But it always made Jack smile, thinking it was the good memories that they shared there that allowed such a small place to have such a big significance. *It's never the place,* he thought to himself, *always the people that make it special.* Soon enough, the familiar sight of Berkeley Fire Station #5 appeared. Jack parked his car and stepped out, pulling his duffel bag from the passenger seat.

"Look who finally decided to show up," Abe called out, raising his coffee mug in mock salute. "Rough night, old man?"

"Something like that," Jack replied, setting his bag down and grabbing a fresh cup of coffee. Abraham joined him at the counter, his voice lowering. "You alright? You've been acting off lately."

Jack shrugged, taking a long sip of his coffee. "Just tired from that trip to Mexico, man. It's a long drive through the desert. I'm good, I promise."

Abe studied him briefly, but whatever he saw in Jack's face made him drop the subject. "Well, you're on hydrant inspections today, so try not to make us look bad. Gotta keep up that "shift of the year" reputation. And I promise you, next week you are not going to Mexico without me." Abe joked, slapping Jack on the shoulder as he walked away.

"Well, I don't really have a choice, do I? We have two fire engines to deliver." Jack managed a weak chuckle, his gaze following Abraham as he disappeared down the hall. The camaraderie of the firehouse felt like a lifeline, but Jack knew it was one he couldn't rely on for much longer if he kept going this way. Too many secrets, too much weight. Still, for now, it was enough to get through the day, and he seemed to manage without raising too much suspicion.

As he pulled on his gear and prepared for his shift, the lighter in his pocket felt heavier than usual. His thoughts flickered back to Ellie, to the fire at the villa, to Calo's innocent young boy. He was terrified that he felt this sense of relief instead of feeling remorse.

"Hey, Jack," - Abe turned back to look at him, "let's grab a beer tomorrow night. You look like you need one."

"You got it." - Jack replied, thinking this wasn't a bad idea after all.

***

Jack and Abe made their way into the Old Brewery - a simple, accommodating local bar that had beer on tap, comfortable, quiet seats, and a good atmosphere. As they walked in, they were hit by the familiar smell of fried food and spilled beer. Jack's been going there since his university days, and made some friends with the staff.

"Jack! I thought you'd moved away, I haven't seen you for ages" - said Bert, the oldest bar staff.

"Been really busy with work, Bert. Always a pleasure to see you!" replied Jack, realizing he has definitely not been enjoying the social life as much as before lately. The thought of hanging out with a group of friends now just seemed overwhelming. He couldn't risk losing focus, couldn't keep building lies on top of lies. Was it all the years of service, the horrors he's seen, or the chaos he has caused himself? *Ah, who cares?* He pushed the dark cloud of thoughts away, acknowledging that he was there to relax and catch up with Abe instead of getting lost in his head again. There's nothing a cold beer and a light-hearted conversation about football can't fix right now.

As they talked, a news segment on the television caught Jack's attention. The screen showed footage of another protest in Berkeley, the crowd chanting slogans against corruption, burning down statues and causing havoc. Some carried signs condemning city officials; others hurled bottles and set fire to trash bins. A shaky clip showed a group tearing down a statue in the center of a small park.

"Here we go again," Abe muttered, shaking his head. "You'd think people would give it a rest."

The news footage panned to a recording of Mayor Quinn, who made a brief statement to reporters, his polished smile giving them a still, cold look. "While I respect the right to peaceful protest, I urge our community to refrain from destructive actions. We are working tirelessly to address your concerns."

Jack let out a sharp breath, his jaw tightening. "Lying bastard."

Abe looked up, surprised by the venom in Jack's voice. "What's that about? You know the guy?"

"I know enough," Jack muttered, his eyes glued to the screen.

The segment shifted, showing aerial footage of the Port of Oakland. The voiceover detailed a drug smuggling investigation that had uncovered ties to cartel activity along the border. Images of cargo containers and law enforcement agents swarming the docks flashed on the screen. Jack's grip on his beer tightened. The sound of the bar seemed to fade, replaced by the pounding of his heart. The Sangre Cartel. It was all connected - Quinn, the port, the cartel's reach is extending farther than anyone realized.

"Jack?" Abe's voice cut through the haze. "You okay?"

Jack blinked, pulling himself back into the moment. "Yeah," he said quickly, sliding out of the booth. "I just remembered something I need to take care of. I'll catch you later."

"Alright, man. Don't work too hard," Abe called after him, his expressive and friendly face giving away his concern.

Jack started to walk away but paused, glancing back. "You ever think this city deserves better than him?"

Abe raised an eyebrow. "The mayor? I mean, yeah, the guy's full of himself, but what politician isn't?"

Jack's eyes darkened. "It's not just ego, Abe. He's rotten, through and through. He's not just ignoring what's happening at the port—he's part of it."

Abe leaned forward, lowering his voice. "That's a heavy accusation, Jack. You got proof, or is this just one of your hunches?"

Jack looked away, his jaw tight. "I just know it."

Abe shook his head, his expression a mix of disbelief and misunderstanding. "You've got to stop letting this stuff get to you. You can put out fires, but you can't save the whole damn city on your own."

Jack gave him a tight smile, a flicker of bitterness in his eyes. "Maybe not. But someone's gotta try."

Before Abe could respond, Jack turned and headed for the door, his mind already racing ahead. Outside, the cool night air hit him like a slap, but it did little to calm the fire raging in his chest.

He knew the Mayor was connected to the cartel. He saw him meeting with Mateo Vargas himself, he just had to wait patiently to prove it. Every second he waited felt like torture, aware that these two men are like an invisible illness - spreading slowly and secretly, until it is too late.

That night, Jack Singer struggled to sleep again, tossing and turning into his own flames of deception.

CHAPTER 2

The first light of dawn hadn't yet pierced the sky over Tijuana when Detective Sofía Calderón's alarm sliced through the silence of her apartment. She blinked into the dim room, her body heavy with exhaustion.

Ever since her brother's death, sleep had become a fleeting luxury, the nights spent tangled in restless memories. She laid in bed for a brief moment, staring at the cracked ceiling she had memorized over countless sleepless hours. But the weight of the day ahead pressed down on her. She swung her legs over the side and planted her feet firmly on the cold floor. Each morning felt like stepping back into an endless battle, but giving up wasn't an option.

As she readied herself for work, her movements were automatic, the routine - a shell to hold her together. She pulled her dark hair back into a tight ponytail, the severe style a mirror to her current mood—grim and focused. In the living room, Rocco was sprawling across the sofa, his ears twitching as he sensed her approach. The loyal German Shepherd was all she had left of her younger brother, Álvaro.

"Hey boy," Sofia murmured, her hand brushing through his thick fur. Rocco looked up with sad, knowing eyes and wagged his tail in a sign of gratitude. "He's not here anymore, but I promise, I'll always be here for you." It was a pledge to the dog, and to herself, a reaffirmation of her duty to protect anyone who is part of the family, no matter the personal cost. She can't make the same mistake twice.

Leaving her apartment, Sofia locked the door behind her and descended into the chilly pre-dawn air. The quiet streets were a stark contrast to the chaos that awaited her at the police department—one that seemed to mirror the turmoil within her. And she was savoring every moment of quiet and peace.

Upon entering the bustling precinct, Sofia was immediately swept up in the day's urgency. Detectives hustled by with files pressed to their chests, phones rang persistently, and the air was thick with the buzz of conversation.

At her desk, a stack of new case files awaited her, a silent testament to the city's never-ending dance with crime.

Sofia poured herself a strong black coffee, the bitter liquid a necessary armor against the day. With the steaming cup in hand, she retreated to her office, a small room with a large window that overlooked the busy street below. It was her own sanctuary within the storm. The walls were lined with evidence of ongoing investigations, the focal point being a large pin board. It was covered in maps, photos of suspects, and various notes scribbled on post-its. In the center, a recent addition: a photograph of Mateo Vargas, a key figure in the Sangre Cartel, marked with a red circle. She knew in her gut he was connected to all the recent fires, but had yet to prove it. A lot of the recent house fires followed a similar pattern, convincing her more and more that the person behind them was experienced and meticulously planned what they were doing. The longer the red question mark on the board was staring at her, the more she convinced herself she was not going to let this go until she knew who was at the heart of this.

Lost in thought, Sofia didn't notice her colleague, Detective Marco Ruiz, standing at her office's doorway. He knocked lightly on the frame to attract her attention—a sound lost in the hum of her focus. When he did it again and was left still without a response, he stepped inside and tapped her on the shoulder.

Startled, Sofia spun around, her hand instinctively reaching for the gun at her hip. "Jesus, Marco, you scared me," she exhaled, her hand clutching her chest as her heart raced.

"Sorry, I didn't mean to interrupt," Marco apologized, with a concerned look on his face. "I knocked, but you didn't hear me. Everything okay?"

Sofia managed a tight smile, her nerves settling. "Yeah, just deep in these cases. What's up?"

Marco hesitated, his eyes scanning her face. "I just wanted to check on you, see how you're holding up. Last night's fire... it brought back some memories, huh?"

Sofia's smile faded, and she turned back to gaze at the pin board, her fingers tracing the edges of Vargas' photo. "Yeah, it did. Every fire does." Her voice was a whisper, lost amidst the echoes of flames that haunted her.

Marco nodded, his expression softening. "Well, I'm here if you need to talk. You know that, right?"

"Thanks, Marco. I appreciate it." Sofia took a deep breath and exhaled slowly, her eyes not leaving the board. "Let's catch this guy. For Álvaro." she said, a silent tribute to her brother, a brave young firefighter who was tragically lost too soon to the very fires she now chased.

Now alone, Sofia was left staring at the board for what felt like forever. As she did so, a recent memory surfaced—a vivid flashback of last night's fire.

***

The blazing fire contrasted starkly with the dark skies, its glow noticeable from miles away. Detective Sofia Calderón drove in and jumped out of her car, her eyes scanning the scene. The air was thick with the acrid scent of charred wood and melted plastic—a suffocating reflection of the night's horrifying events. Local firefighters worked tirelessly, dousing the last stubborn embers at what used to be a once-grand villa on the outskirts of Ensenada. Yellow tape fluttered in the breeze as her team meticulously combed through the ashes, searching for any clue that might reveal the cause of the fire.

Sofia stepped carefully over the wreckage, her boots crunching on the scorched debris. The forensic anthropologist was crouched nearby, careful- ly brushing soot from a small fragment. He glanced up as she approached, his face pale and tight.

"Detective," he began, his voice subdued. "It's bad. It appears there was a whole family inside when the fire started." He gestured toward a small collection of bone fragments laid out on a tarp. "We've found what's left of some skeletal remains amongst the ashes—three bodies, or what's left of them."

Sofia knelt beside him, her stomach twisting as she looked at the bones. "A family?" she asked, her voice low. Amongst the charred remains, something caught her eye—tiny fragments of bone, barely distinguishable from the debris.

The forensic anthropologist nodded grimly. "This was no accident. Whoever did this used fire accelerants—likely propane or butane, as these are odorless and less likely to alert the family to their presence. The flames burned hotter and longer than normal, leaving almost nothing behind. There's hardly anything left, but…" He hesitated, picking up a tiny fragment of bone. "This here, Detective… It's from a child. By the size and development, I'd say it was around ten years old."

Sofia stared at the fragment in his hand, her throat tightening. The image of a young boy flashed in her mind—a life snuffed out in unimaginable horror. She swallowed hard, trying to suppress the wave of emotions rising in her chest. "What kind of monster would do this?" she muttered under her breath, her voice trembling with sorrow, her clenched fists giving away her barely contained rage.

The anthropologist didn't reply, his eyes fixed on the ground. This was nothing short of the usual for him. Sofia straightened, her gaze sweeping over the charred remains of the villa. The air felt heavier now, thick not just with smoke but with the weight of an unspoken tragedy.

"Sofia, I think you might want to see this."

"What is it?" Sofia asked, standing as he came closer.

Marco approached, holding out a charred, half-burned photograph, its edges blackened and curling inward. The image was faint but visible—a family, smiling, their faces obscured by soot and damage.

"It looks like some kind of family picture." Sofia said softly, her voice tinged with both curiosity and unease. She reached out but hesitated, letting Marco continue to hold it. "Where did you find this?"

"Over there," Marco said, tilting his head toward the far side of the room. "Near what used to be the fireplace, I think. I am surprised a remnant of this survived, to be quite honest."

Sofia watched intently, her professional detachment giving way to a flicker of adrenaline. "Get this to the lab. I need to know who these people are," she instructed, carefully handing back the photo.

Marco nodded and carefully tucked the fragile photo into an evidence bag. Sofia's gaze lingered on the fireplace, now nothing more than charred rubble. Her mind raced, piecing together the puzzle of the scene before her.

"This wasn't just a fire," she said finally, her voice firm despite the emotion simmering beneath. "It was a message."

The investigator beside her nodded solemnly. "Deliberate and merciless. Whoever did this wanted to erase this family from existence."

She turned to her team; her resolve hardening. "I want a full report on the accelerants. Check for anything unusual—tools, chemicals, footprints. And get me a list of anyone who might've had a reason to target this family. I want to know who did this, and I want to know why."

Sofia's eyes burned as she turned to take in the full devastation once more.

The fire had not only consumed the structure but also erased nearly all traces of the lives that once thrived there. Now, all that remained was the smell of smoke and a lingering heat that seemed to emanate from the blackened ground. With that, she turned back toward the remnants of the villa, her boots crunching on scorched debris as her mind raced with possibilities.

***

Sofia snapped back to the present, the image of the fire still vivid in her mind. The weight of last night's events pressed heavily on her shoulders as she pinned the new evidence to the board. The smoky scent seemed to cling to her, a constant reminder of the tragedy that had unfolded - and a painful reminder of her own loss.

That night, like many before, Sofia worked late. The precinct had quieted down, the buzz of activity reduced to the occasional shuffle of night shift officers and the distant hum of city life. It was easier for her to concentrate when she was embraced by silence.

Alone in her office, she revisited the evidence, her mind tirelessly turning over each detail. The pattern was clear, and her gut told her there was more to these incidents than faulty wiring or neglected campfires - this was planned, and the fire always started in the center of the house, spreading quickly and bringing death and destruction with it. Each blaze had occurred near properties rumored to be connected to the Sangre Cartel, and each left little behind but ashes and questions.

Hours later, her phone buzzed. It was the forensic analyst, a wiry man with a sharp eye for detail and a knack for uncovering hidden truths. "Sofia, you might want to see this," he said, his voice a mix of excitement and disbelief.

The streets were nearly empty as she drove to the lab, the silence of the night punctuated only by the occasional siren in the distance.

Upon arrival, the analyst greeted her with a thick folder of reports and a serious expression. "We managed to enhance the image," he said, leading her to his workstation. On the screen, the photo was displayed in sharp detail. While the faces were still unrecognizable, a striking detail emerged: a tattoo on the forearm of one of the figures. It was intricate, almost ornamental, a serpent coiled tightly around a dagger.

Sofia leaned closer, her brow furrowing. "That's... unusual. Did you get any matches?"

The analyst shook his head, his tone grim. "I've run it through every database we have access to—gang markers, military insignias, even obscure art collections. Nothing. It's like whoever this is didn't want to be found."

Sofia's fingers tapped against the edge of the workstation as she studied the image. Her mind raced. Was the tattoo a personal emblem, or did it symbolize something far more sinister? The lack of a match only made it more unsettling.

"Keep digging," she said finally, her voice steady despite the tension in her chest. "Someone went to a lot of trouble to make sure they'd stay invisible. I need to know why."

She immediately called him back. "What's going on, Marco?" she asked, her voice sharp with concern.

"We finally got in touch with the real estate agents," Marco began, his tone heavy. "They said the house was bought in cash—no loans, no paper trail. They never even met the buyers in person. It was all handled through a third party." Sofia's brow furrowed as Marco continued, "It gets worse. We dug into the name the property is registered under, but it's a dead end. The name doesn't exist in any official records. No ID, no tax filings, no nothing. Whoever owns that house is a ghost."

Her grip on the phone tightened. "A ghost who didn't want to be found," she muttered, her mind racing. The deeper they went, the darker the puzzle seemed to grow.

"Exactly," Marco said. "I'll fill you in tomorrow at the meeting. But Sofia—this whole thing, it's starting to feel bigger than we thought."

She ended the call and stared at her phone for a moment, the knot in her stomach tightening further. Every lead they had seemed designed to vanish into thin air, leaving behind nothing but questions and shadows.

As she prepared to leave, another piece of evidence caught her eye—a partial fingerprint lifted from the photo. She froze, the implications swirling in her mind. "Run this through every database we have," she instructed the analyst. "And check for any cross-matches internationally. I have a feeling we're dealing with more than just local thugs."

Hours later, her phone rang. The analyst's voice on the other end sounded hesitant. "Detective, we got a hit," the analyst said. "You're not going to like this."

Her stomach sank. "Whose is it?"

"It's... your brother, Álvaro," he replied quietly.

Sofia felt the floor tilt beneath her. Álvaro? That couldn't be right. "That doesn't make sense," she said sharply. "How would his fingerprint end up on a photo in that house? He's been gone for over a year."

"We double-checked the system. It's him. But here's the thing—firefighters sometimes do inspections on properties like this, right? Could that explain it?"

Her mind raced, grasping for context. Álvaro had mentioned going out for inspections weeks ago, but never this house. She racked her brain, piecing it together. "Check the records. Was anyone with him that day?" she asked, her voice steady but tinged with urgency.

The analyst hesitated. "There's no record of anyone else. But if you want to dig into the inspection logs..."

Sofia didn't wait. She pulled up her own access to the department's records, her fingers flying over the keyboard. Within moments, the inspection logs appeared on the screen, and her heart sank as she scanned the entries. Álvaro's name was there, tied to an inspection of the villa nearly a month before his death. She stared at the record, unease prickling at the back of her neck. "He was on the inspection logs for that property," she murmured, almost to herself. "Could this fingerprint have come from that visit?"

"It's possible," the analyst admitted.

"But if that's the case, we're missing something. Who else was with him? And why wasn't anything flagged about the property before now?"

Álvaro had always been by the book, meticulous with his work. If there had been anything unusual about that inspection, he would have said something—wouldn't he? The fingerprint told her that much, but it was a detail without context, and that made it worse. *Perhaps I am making this up, and it's just an odd coincidence.*

"Keep looking," she said finally, her voice steady despite the storm inside her. "See if you can find anything else—maintenance logs, reports, anything from that time."

As she ended the call, her mind reeled. If Álvaro had been at the villa officially, why had his involvement led to nothing? Who else had been with him? And more importantly, what had they seen—or missed? The answers felt buried as deeply as the ashes of the villa itself, but one thing was becoming clear: whoever had orchestrated this fire had ties to her brother's past.

She sat back in her chair, the room silent except for the hum of her computer. Her eyes lingered on the inspection log. Álvaro's name was there, as plain as day, yet the entry told her nothing. Her gaze drifted to the photo resting in its evidence bag on the desk, the partial fingerprint glaring back at her like a silent accusation. The weight of it pressed down on her—a clue without answers, a question without context. The villa was full of ghosts, and now it felt like Álvaro was one of them. But she knew better than to chase shadows. She stood and crossed to the evidence board, her fingers brushing over the photos pinned in place. The villa, the burned photograph, the tattoo. Each piece was a fragment of a puzzle that refused to come together. Her brother's connection to the villa might explain the fingerprint, but it didn't explain the fire—or the deliberate destruction it had left behind.

Her eyes narrowed, and she grabbed a marker, circling the villa on the board. Next to it, she scrawled a single word: *Why?*

The soft creak of the floor behind her snapped her attention to the doorway, but it was empty. Her nerves, frayed by hours of piecing together scraps of information, were starting to play tricks on her. She shook her head and exhaled, forcing herself to refocus.

"Paranoia's a hell of a thing," she muttered under her breath, shaking her head. But as she reached to switch off her computer, she hesitated, her fingers hovering over the keyboard. Instead, she opened the villa's records one more time, her instincts refusing to let go.

The inspection. The photo. The fire. The unanswered questions it left behind.

The pieces didn't add up. And she had a feeling they weren't meant to. And the more she thought about it, the more she realized the fire wasn't meant to be the end of something. It was the beginning.

CHAPTER 3

The fire station was alive with its usual morning rhythm: coffee brewing in the corner, the hum of light-hearted banter, and the occasional clatter of gear being loaded into trucks. It was a nice, sunny day in Berkeley, and the air smelled of excitement and a touch of salt brought by the gentle breeze. Jack stood by the engine, quietly double-checking their equipment. His eyes scanned each item, lingering on the donations bound for the Los Fuegos Crew in Mexico—fire hoses, masks, axes, and other surplus gear.

He hadn't forgotten the conversation he'd had with Abe last week in that bar - hoping that he had. Jack admitted to himself he had one beer too many and showed too much emotion - *"You must control your emotions better. Remember that you owe them, not them - you. Otherwise, you are not cut out for this job"* - his mentor Xavier would always say to him, his voice now echoing in his head.

Abe showed up in his usual boisterous self, excited about the upcoming trip to Mexico. "A chance to do some good and soak up the sun? Count me in!" Abe said, flashing his easy grin.

Jack nodded along, masking his real purpose for the trip. Now, standing here with the weight of his double life pressing down on him, the reality of what lay ahead felt heavier than the gear he was about to carry. In his pocket, he had a name and an address, written in black on a lined paper sheet, pulled out of a pocket journal - ironically looking like a grocery list. A list that he will destroy in the fire he is about to start, along with every other evidence - be it human or not. Last night, after tucking Ellie goodnight, he loaded the map of the location and accessed satellite footage on his computer to cross-check all of his information about the next victim's house - the entry points, the structural vulnerabilities, the proximity of neighboring buildings. He had planned everything ahead. His visit to Ensenada earlier this month was more than a cold-blooded murder. It was all part of his preparation for the next hit; a complex calculation of how much butane he needs, the most vulnerable location in the house, and the ideal timing for the fire to start. To ensure he has enough time to escape, he invented his own timed ignition device - a lit cigarette taped to a match bundle, wrapped in paper. This gave him enough time to leave the premises undetected. He wasn't a smoker, but he would always light one up after each arson - he liked the irony of joining in with the smoke, one fire taking away life faster than the other. His years of experience as a firefighter equipped him with all the helpful knowledge he needed - knowing what ceased and caused a fire, and the sure ways to make them deadly.

"Jack, you ready for this? Los Cerros, here we come!" - Abe interrupted his train of busy thoughts.

Jack managed a faint smile. "Yeah, just making sure everything's in order."

"Man, you're like a checklist come to life," Abe joked, tossing a small bag into the truck. "Relax, we're just delivering some gear. What can go wrong? Forget an extra hose? I am sure they've managed without it so far."

"Yeah, you are right," Jack tried to put a relaxed face on, his gaze drifting to the black duffel bag tucked neatly in the corner of the truck bed. Inside was everything he needed for his other mission—the one Abe could never know about.

As they each climbed into their truck and pulled out of the station, Abe pulled his window down, aviator sunglasses on and a grin spreading from his left to his right ear. "You ever think about how weird it is, doing these trips?"

Jack glanced at him. "What do you mean?"

Abe shrugged. "I mean, don't get me wrong, I love helping out, but sometimes it feels like we're just slapping band-aids on problems no one's fixing. These guys in Mexico—what do they even do when we're not around?"

Jack gripped the wheel a little tighter. "They make do. Like we all do."

Abe didn't notice the edge in his voice. "Yeah, well, I'm just glad we're giving them the good stuff this time. That old gear we hauled last year was falling apart."

Jack nodded, thinking that the upcoming mission had to go perfectly. Mateo Vargas, the cartel enforcer, would be nearby, and Jack had a chance to cripple their operations and finally commit to the beginning of the end of Vargas. God knows how much he hated the guy, after everything he has done - all the drug smuggling, human trafficking, all the pain and death he has brought all the way to Berkeley. It had to stop, even though he was warned to thread carefully with Vargas. "What are they going to do, fire me?" he thought to himself, finding the idea amusing and even a little tempting.

***

The drive was long. The terrain shifting from smooth highways to dusty back roads.

"Man, I'll tell you," Abe said, wiping his brow with a gloved hand, "next time we do a charity run, let's pick somewhere with a little less heat. Like Alaska." By the time they reached Los Cerros, the sun hung low in the sky, casting the village in golden light. The air was dry and heavy, carrying the faint scent of smoke and dust, a particular smell of a place that is half a desert.

The Los Fuegos Crew greeted them warmly, their leader, Carlos, shaking hands firmly with both Jack and Abe. "It's good to see you again, Jack," Carlos said, his weathered face splitting into a smile. "Your help means the world to us."

Abe grinned, already launching into conversation with the younger firefighters, swapping stories about the craziest calls they'd answered back in Berkeley. Jack joined in but stayed quieter, his eyes scanning the outskirts of the village.

He noticed the black SUV parked at the edge of the square, sticking out like a sore thumb in these humble surroundings. Its windows were tinted, and its engine idled for a moment before it pulled away, kicking up dust. *They know,* Jack thought. *How could they know?* He was certain these were Matteo Vargas' men, tracking him down. Either that or it is a huge coincidence. And Jack Singer didn't believe in coincidences.

Carlos had good connections in the village, and arranged a nice B&B for the boys - they couldn't drive all this way back, and of course that plan wouldn't work. For Jack - because he had a greater purpose on his mind, and for Abe - because he wanted to make the most out of it. The village was quiet that night, save for the occasional bark of a dog or the faint sound of laughter. Jack and Abe had eaten a simple meal and retired early to their shared room in the guesthouse.

Abe sat on his bed, scrolling through his phone. "Man, this place is something else. The houses, the roads, the people - it's like time stopped here."

Jack glanced up briefly from the map spread out on the desk. "Yeah, it's got charm," he said, though his tone lacked conviction.

Abe snorted. "Charm, huh? You mean the kind where you half-expect a tumbleweed to roll by and a guy on horseback to challenge you to a duel?" He shook his head, chuckling. "I swear, Jack, sometimes I think you could live in a place like this. At least the firemen are constantly busy with all the heat."

Jack folded one edge of the map, keeping his eyes on the desk. "Maybe. Quiet has its perks. Plus, there is a lot of nature to explore. Ain't that peaceful?"

Abe set his phone down, leaning back against the headboard. "Quiet. You?" He laughed. Man, I don't know. I remember when you used to be the life of the firehouse. And when you and Jen got together, you both agreed you enjoyed the city life and wanted to settle there. What happened to you, old man?"

"I think what happened to Jen...it changed me. The job changed me. Witnessing all these people die... you know how it is. Plus, I have had a lot going on lately. Anyway, why don't you try and get some sleep? I will go get some fresh air for 5 minutes and will hit the pillow, too. It's been a long d ay."

Abe studied him for a moment, then sighed. "Fair enough, man. Just don't let all that 'quiet charm' swallow you whole. You've got people who care, you know, talk to us."

Jack's hand paused briefly over the zipper of the duffel bag, but he didn't look up. "I know," he said simply. In a matter of a few quiet minutes he heard Abe's snoring - "Like clockwork" he thought, knowing this is his sign to move. He convinced Abe they should have an extra glass of wine at dinner, hoping this will put him to sleep, and luckily, he didn't need much convincing. Jack grabbed his duffle bag, hesitating for a moment and throwing a cautious look at his sleeping friend, then slipped quietly out into the night and picked up his burner phone to make a single phone call. "You know what to do," said the voice on the other side.

Jack knew that a successful day starts the night before and not planning everything to the smallest detail was a risk. Even with the perfect plan, there were risks involved, Jack thought, wondering how much longer he could survive this duality. The air was thick with the scent of salt and dust as he crept through the dimly lit streets, occasionally seeing a couple of young Mexican guys sipping on beer by the pavement. The village of Los Cerros was unlike any other place Jack had visited. It was tucked along the Rio Grande, just a few miles south of the U.S.-Mexico border, and it had this charming rugged look, borne of resilience. He walked by a house and couldn't help but have a glimpse inside - the curtains were open; the room bathed in warm candlelight. He saw a man and his family having dinner, and he thought about how much he missed Ellie. The man picked up his daughter's plate and gave her a peck on the forehead. Could he live a normal, simple life like this, too? Was he even capable of it?

The men who lived here were not simple farmers, he thought as he looked at that dad. They were brave firefighters, members of the Los Fuegos Crew - a cross-border team that often fought big fires and helped the U.S. crews, too.

Jack had met some of them during his last charity run. Their operation was impressive, if unconventional. When the U.S. National Park Service needed them for the big fire of August 2023, the Los Fuegos Crew would cross the Rio Grande, sometimes wading through its shallows or rowing in their boats, to battle the big flames in the Big Bend National Park. The village had become an essential stop on Jack's trips, where his work as a firefighter helped him blend in, and no one suspected that he had a different side of him, one that felt like it was at war. Tonight, Los Cerros was more than just a waypoint—it was the stage for his next operation. As he moved closer to the outskirts of the village, he was surrounded by silence - save for the occasional bark of a stray dog or the distant hum of cicadas. Jack started moving swiftly, making his way by the dusty paths that snaked between old houses overlooking the fields. The Los Fuegos Crew was busy preparing for the dry season, which always brought with it the threat of wildfires. Jack and Abe spent their afternoon with them, sharing tips, putting the donated equipment away, and telling stories over cold cervezas. Though he knew how to play the game and genuinely liked these fellows, beneath the smiles and camaraderie, his mind was elsewhere-focused on the safehouse at the edge of town.

His target was an old, nondescript building, perfectly blending into its surroundings like a predator in the brush. Jack knew he had to be vigilant: the place was marked as a key hub for the Sangre Cartel, notorious for smuggling drugs across the border. Worse, it was one of the known haunts of Mateo Vargas, the cartel's enforcer, the man Jack hated more than anyone else. Under the cover of night, Jack approached the back of the house with his duffel bag slung over his shoulder. He moved with the ease of a man who had done this before, every step calculated, every movement deliberate. The sound of laughter drifted from within, accompanied by the occasional clink of bottles. Jack's jaw tightened.

Mateo Vargas had been the reason for so much pain, so much destruction and chaos. He was more than a criminal; he was a ghost, always one step ahead of him. Tonight, though, Mateo wasn't supposed to be here. Jack had ensured the intel pointed elsewhere. Still, he couldn't shake the feeling of being watched ever since he saw that black SUV.

***

The midday sun bathed Los Cerros in a soft golden glow as Jack and Abe arrived at the small fire station to bid farewell to the Los Fuegos Crew. The village was already stirring with life, locals bustling about their morning routines - a huge contrast to the quiet evenings.

Carlos greeted the boys warmly as they arrived, "Jack, Abe! Come, sit. We've got coffee brewing," he said, gesturing to a modest table surrounded by mismatched chairs.

Abe plopped into a chair with his usual easygoing grin. "Don't mind if I do. Let me guess—this is the good stuff, right? None of that instant powder?"

Carlos chuckled. "Only the best!"

Jack sat beside Abe, his demeanor quieter but polite. As the crew passed around mugs and offered thanks for the donated equipment, Jack listened to their stories, smiling faintly at their enthusiasm. There have been a lot more fires lately, not just because of the hot climate - someone's been intentionally setting houses on fire, taking many victims. "Good to see the gear's working out," Jack said, his voice steady but distant. He couldn't help but think that he might be the one responsible for the majority of these fires. Abe noticed Jack's distraction and nudged him playfully. "Hey, don't look so serious. You're making me look bad—like I don't care about all this hard work we did."

Jack smirked, sipping his coffee. "Somebody's gotta balance you out."

Just as they were preparing to leave, the station's radio crackled to life. A tense voice came over the line, speaking rapid Spanish. Carlos' expression darkened as he listened, his eyes darting toward the hills visible beyond the station's open doors.

"Grass fire," Carlos said grimly, addressing his crew. "It's moving fast. We'll need all hands on this one."

Abe groaned, leaning against the truck. "What kind of idiot sets fires in this heat? It's like asking for trouble."

Jack's jaw tightened, his expression unreadable. "These fires aren't always accidental," he said softly, almost to himself.

"Doesn't matter. Let's suit up. We're here. Might as well help." - Abe said, feeling a rush of excitement and adrenaline.

Minutes later, Jack and Abe joined the Los Fuegos Crew on the narrow dirt road leading into the hills. The orange flames were already visible in the distance, the air thick with heat and the acrid scent of burning vegetation. The rising smoke cast a hazy shadow over the village below.

Abe coughed, adjusting his helmet. "Man, I don't envy you guys. This heat's worse than any house fire we get back home."

While everyone was occupied with the fire, Jack remained focused, his eyes scanning the terrain as they approached the fire line. He recognized the telltale patterns of a deliberately set blaze: the way it spread unevenly, jumping between patches of dry grass. It wasn't random - this was all part of his plan. The distraction had worked perfectly, drawing the local firefighters away from the safe house - his main target.

"Abe," Jack called, pointing downhill toward a cluster of smoldering patches. "I'm going to check for flare-ups. Stay here and keep this line clear."

Abe nodded, wiping sweat from his brow. "Be careful, man. This thing's got a mind of its own."

Jack didn't respond as he moved downhill, his steps deliberate but quick. Once he was out of sight, he veered off the fire line, heading toward an abandoned shed he had scouted the night before. The structure was barely standing, its weathered wood blackened by time and heat.

Behind the shed, hidden beneath a loose board, was the duffel bag he had planted the previous night. Jack crouched and pulled it free, the weight of its contents reassuring in his hands. He unzipped it quickly, grabbed his gun and the remote control connected to the incendiary device. The target safehouse was only a few yards away now, just behind this hill. He strategically started that wildfire to keep everyone busy and distracted, looking away from the house.

Jack worked swiftly. The incendiary device—a timed creation using a lit cigarette, matches, and accelerant—was designed to ignite precisely when he needed it to with the press of a button, blasting the invisible layer of odorless butane. He double-checked the setup, his hands steady despite the tension in his chest. This hit will show Vargas that he needs to stop digging into other people's business.

"This has to work," he muttered to himself, the words as much a prayer as a promise, as he pressed the button, letting Vargas' safehouse be consumed by flames, taking everyone inside with them and leaving nothing but destruction behind.

Chapter 4

The drive back from Los Cerros was long and quiet, with the vast expanse of desert rolling out like a golden-brown quilt under the midday sun. The pickup truck Jack got offered from the bomberos to get home hummed steadily along the highway, the Mexican border now miles behind them. It was his turn to drive, and Abe sat in the passenger seat, leaning against the window, his face full of exhaustion. Jack knew he was exhausted when he didn't hear a joke from him for a while. The trip had been draining—the heat, the fires, and the endless hiding.

"Next time, remind me to bring a portable air conditioner," Abe muttered without opening his eyes. "Or at least one of those tiny fans."

Jack managed a faint smile, gripping the steering wheel a little tighter. "I'll make sure to add it to the gear list," he replied, though his mind was miles away. The hum of the truck engine blended into the rhythm of his thoughts, a cacophony of guilt, precision, and a grim sense of purpose. He couldn't stop picturing the fire that blazed through the hills of Los Cerros, its light reflecting in the dark windows of the quiet Mexican village. That fire wasn't just an inferno—it was a message, sharp and brutal, meant to pierce the heart of Mateo Vargas. Jack's mind returned to the safehouse. He replayed every detail in his head like a film reel: the device he planted, the moment it ignited, the roar of flames consuming everything in its path. Had it worked? Would the destruction be enough to make Vargas reconsider his movements? He thought of Vargas's cousin, a trusted crew member who was inside when the blaze began. Jack had calculated every risk, knowing this strike would cut deeper than most. He hoped it would be enough to force Vargas into a retreat, buying time—time for Ellie, for Berkeley, for the world Jack was still trying to protect. For a brief moment, Jack allowed himself to hope. Maybe this was the beginning of the end. Maybe he could finally finish this mission, put the Sangre Cartel in his rearview mirror, and find a way back to a life that felt real. He thought of Ellie, of her bright eyes and the way she still waited up for him, even when she pretended not to. He thought of the promises he made silently in the dark: to be there for her, to make up for the void Jen's absence left behind.

"No, no, there is more...Stop!" Abe's voice broke through his haze, poor fellow talking in his sleep.

Jack blinked, glancing briefly at his friend. "Abe," he said, half-whispering. "Abe, you're having a nightmare."

Abe half-opened his eyes and chuckled, shaking his head. "Wow, I must have dozed off. When did that happen? Didn't know I was capable of falling asleep in a truck, not with you behind the wheel anyway."

"Very funny," Jack said, his gaze fixed on the horizon. The border was behind them, but the weight of his choices felt as heavy as ever, pressing down on his chest like the heat of the fires he both fought and started. As the miles stretched ahead, the tension coiled tighter within him. The mission was far from over, and Jack knew better than anyone that the worst was yet to come.

***

Ellie was waiting on the front steps of her aunt Megan's house when Jack arrived.

"Hey, kiddo," he said softly, pulling her into a hug. "I missed you," she mumbled into his chest.

"I missed you too," Jack replied, his voice heavy with guilt. He ruffled her hair and pulled back, studying her face. "Everything okay?"

Ellie shrugged, glancing toward the house. "Aunt Meghan was nice...I managed to win a game of scrabble against uncle Peter last night! Can we just go home now?"

Jack nodded, sensing there was more she wanted to say but wasn't ready to. Meg appeared in the doorway, giving Jack a small wave.

"Hey Jack," she said, her face forever tainted with a sense of lingering blame and disappointment. She still couldn't help but blame Jack for Jen's death. She loved her sister and would do anything to bring her back. Losing Jen crushed her more than anything, and now she has to live with it. Every day. More than just a sibling, Jen was Meghan's best friend, her older protector, her light shining even on the darkest of days. They worked together and spent many weekends having fun together. Now, Ellie was the closest thing she had left from Jen, and despite her and Peter not having children, she cherished every moment spent with Ellie.

"How are you, Meg? How's Peter?" - Jack asked, exchanging the usual pleasantries out of obligation and respect, not because he really needed to know.

"We're good, thanks. And how are things going for you, Jack? Is the job still so demanding?"

"Well, you know how it is. There is always something going on in Oakland."

Meghan frowned, crossing her arms. "You know, Ellie talks to me when she's here. She mentioned skipping homework last week. Jack, are you sure you're keeping an eye on her?"

The words stung more than they should have. "I'm doing the best I can, Meghan. It's not easy, you know that."

"I do," she said softly, but her tone carried an edge. "I'm just saying... maybe she needs more stability. She's been through so much, and with you always gone—"

Jack's jaw tightened. "I'm not always gone."

There was a brief moment of awkward silence and a tension built up from all the things left unsaid. Jack knew what she was thinking, but she didn't know what he was *actually* going through. Nobody knew. How could they? Maybe that is why men struggle to talk about how they actually feel... They are expected to always seize the day and succeed in every area of their lives. But very few people actually care to ask what is going on underneath that mask of bravery they are wearing.

"She's a good kid. Look after her, Jack." Meg said, her voice putting an end to their shared discomfort.

"Thanks for keeping an eye on her," Jack replied. He didn't linger a moment longer than he had to. He just wanted to get Ellie home.

"Don't be afraid to ask for help, Jack." - Meghan's voice echoed behind him, as he and Ellie walked to the car. As they were leaving the Elmwood neighborhood, they cruised past many big, seemingly peaceful homes with white picket fences on their way back to Jack and Ellie's terrace home. It started pouring down with rain.

The rain and driving down this familiar road made Jack's thoughts drift, unbidden, to the day his life shattered. It wasn't a memory he often summoned, but it crept up on him in quiet moments like this, when the world outside felt too still.

It had been a rainy evening, the kind where water pooled on the windshield faster than wipers could clear it. Jack was halfway through a long shift at the station when the call came in—an accident on the interstate. His mind barely registered the details at first: a sedan crushed beneath the weight of a truck, multiple injuries reported. Just another call, he had thought, another crisis to handle. Sounded pretty bad, but nothing he hadn't seen before. But as they neared the scene, his stomach dropped. Even from a distance, he recognized the car—a familiar silver sedan, the one he drove almost every day. The one Jen had borrowed that night because hers had been in the shop. He was praying to be wrong, and even while running towards it, he kept on saying, "It can't be. You're making this up. You're just paranoid." Jack's breath caught as the flashing lights illuminated the wreckage.

The sedan was barely recognizable, its frame twisted and crumpled beneath the massive truck. Rain slicked the pavement, and the air smelled of scorched rubber and gasoline. He barely remembered jumping out of the firetruck. The chaos around him blurred: shouts from the other responders, the shrill whine of sirens, the crunch of debris under his feet. His entire focus was on getting to the driver's seat, on finding her. Jen was slumped against the airbag, her face pale and streaked with blood. The truck had slammed into the driver's side, leaving little chance for her to brace herself. Jack shouted her name, his voice breaking as he reached for her, but she didn't respond. The paramedics and firefighters pulled him back, their voices calm but firm, telling him he couldn't help here. "Jack, we got this. Please give us some space." He stumbled away, watching helplessly as they pried the door open and carefully extricated her from the wreckage.

Later, at the hospital, they told him she didn't make it. Severe internal injuries. Too much blood loss. They had done everything they could, but the impact had been too devastating. Jack hadn't been able to process it at first. All he could think about was how it should've been him. It had been his car. He had been the one who was supposed to drive it that day. He was ready to bargain for her life, but no one was listening. And now all he was left with was a life filled with stark solitude as a single-parent and a double-agent.

The sight of her car, crumpled like a discarded can, was burned into his memory, the ashes carrying the stench of despair and the overwhelming color of grief. He hadn't been able to save her, and that failure haunted him every day.

He blinked back the memory, checking on Ellie, who was also staring at the raindrops running down the car's window, lost in her own little world. Jack was hoping that she was in a better space than he was when she went into her head. *Ah, who am I kidding...*Jen's absence was a gaping hole in their lives, and no matter how hard he tried, he couldn't fill it.

Once they got home, Jack helped Ellie unpack, and they both gave each other some space. "Let's have dinner around 7, okay, kiddo? I'll make you your favorite."

"Lasagna?" Ellie asked in excitement.

"You know it," replied Jack, finally feeling like he can do something for her that brings her joy.

***

Ellie seemed distracted at dinner, reaching for her phone every time it buzzed with a new text from one of her friends.

"Ellie, you know how rude it is to use your phone at the table. What's so important that you can't spend 30 minutes with your old man, eh?" Jack said, trying to keep a calm tone and be friendly. He was afraid she might shut him off otherwise.

His daughter blushed and muttered, "Nothing. Sorry, dad. Didn't mean to ignore you."

Jack's instincts as a father and his experience taught him one thing - to be able to trust his gut. And his gut was telling him Ellie was up to no good. She pushed her phone aside and focused on her plate, though her facial expression remained guilty. Jack watched her for a moment, his fork resting idly in his hand. The more she grew up, the more obvious it became to him that she had Jen's eyes—the same warmth, the same spark—but lately, that spark seemed distant, dimmed by something Jack couldn't quite place. She was soon to turn fourteen. Maybe that's what it was. Maybe there was a boy messing with her head? He wanted to tell her to be safe, but where does he even start, and what would be the best way to not come across as controlling? He tried to shake the feeling. Maybe it was normal teenage behavior. Maybe he was overthinking it, like Meghan always said.

But that little voice inside him, the one that had kept him alive through countless fires and dangerous missions, whispered that something wasn't right.

"So," Jack broke the silence as he twirled his fork in the remains of the lasagna he had prepared—its once comforting aroma of basil and tomato now a fading backdrop. "How's school? Any big projects coming up?" he asked, trying to bridge the gap between them.

Ellie shrugged. "Not really. Just the usual stuff."

Jack waited, hoping she'd elaborate, but she didn't. "You know," he said, keeping his tone light, "your mom always used to say I wasn't allowed to talk about work at the table. Said it ruined the mood."

Ellie looked up, a faint smile tugging at her lips. "Yeah, she'd tell me the same thing when I complained about homework."

Jack chuckled softly, the memory of Jen's gentle scolding momentarily easing the tension. "Smart lady, your mom."

"Yeah," Ellie said quietly, her gaze dropping back to her plate.

Jack noticed the disconnect between them. It seemed that every time he went away; he came back to a more distant daughter, one that was growing up so fast, and didn't trust him enough to share much with him. As they talked, the faint sounds of crickets chirping outside blended with the occasional car passing by in the otherwise quiet neighborhood. The crisp summer breeze wafted in through the open window above the sink, mingling with the lingering scent of lasagna. The warm lighting in the kitchen cast a cozy glow, adding a comforting sense of normalcy.

After dinner, Ellie retreated to her room, leaving Jack alone in the kitchen. While he was drying the plates with a soft, cotton dish towel—the fabric gentle against his hands and slightly damp from use—it was one he had given to his wife years ago. Each touch of the cloth reminded him of better times, even as his mind kept drifting back to the message on his phone. *Safehouse confirmed. Target eliminated.* Mateo Vargas was closer to breaking, closer to slipping up. But with every move Jack made, the risks grew higher—not just for him, but for Ellie, too. He set the last dish on the rack and wiped his hands on a towel. The house was quiet, save for the faint sound of music coming from Ellie's room. Jack leaned against the counter, his gaze drifting to the photo of Jen on the mantle. "What would you do, Jen?" he murmured. "Am I doing this right? Am I doing enough for her?"

The only answer was the faint hum of the refrigerator.

Around midnight, Jack found himself lying awake in bed, staring at the ceiling. The rain had picked up again, pattering softly against the windows. Ellie's door was closed, the faint glow of her lamp spilling into the hallway. He couldn't shake the nagging feeling in his chest. Ellie had been distracted all through dinner, her phone buzzing incessantly. It wasn't just the texting—it was the way she reacted, the way she tried to hide her smile, the way her blush deepened when he asked about it. He swung his legs over the side of the bed and sat up, running a hand through his hair. Maybe he was being paranoid, but he needed to be sure. Quietly, he padded down the hall and knocked lightly on Ellie's door.

"Ellie?"

No response.

He knocked again. "Ellie, you awake?"

Still nothing. Concern furrowed his brow as he opened the door just enough to peek inside. Her bed was empty, the covers pushed to one side. The window was slightly ajar; the curtains swaying gently in the breeze.

Jack's heart dropped.

"Hey, dad, why are you up?", said Ellie, appearing what seemed out of the blue.

"Oh, my God, Ellie, you scared the life out of me!" he exclaimed, relief washing over him.

"Relax, dad, I was just using the bathroom. Stop being so paranoid."

Jack shut her window, tucked her to sleep and went back to his bedroom, his body still carrying the sense of anxiety and adrenaline. "Jesus, Jack, get your shit together. You're being paranoid again. No one knows who you are. Nothing can happen to her." - Jack repeated to himself, his voice nothing but a brief whisper, his words almost a prayer. That night, like many others, Jack couldn't sleep, drowning in memories of distant screams, fires, and the duality of saving and taking lives. He reached out for his prescription pills, knowing that he will regret it in the morning. At this point, he was desperate to get some peaceful shuteye, and willing to pay the price.

Chapter 5

On a sunny morning in Tijuana, Sofia decided to take an unusual break from the relentless pace of her work and her routine. She sat on a quiet bench, unleashed Rocco with a gentle "off you go", and watched him playfully chase the squirrels darting from tree to tree - a scene of domestic bliss that she seldom enjoys. The park is lively yet serene, with ducks swimming in the nearby lake and people rowing boats gently across the water, the soft splashes blending with children's giggles. With a steaming cup of coffee in hand, she takes in the surrounding scene like a breath of fresh air: families laughing together, children playing, and friends chatting, feeling a pang of envy for their normalcy—a stark contrast to her own life consumed by her relentless pursuit of justice. For a fleeting moment, she yearned for simplicity and peace that seemed to flow effortlessly around her. *Could this be my life?*, she wondered silently. Yet, as quickly as the thought came, it vanished, replaced by a deep-seated conviction. *No, I vowed to make a difference. I walk this path not just for me, but for those who can't fight for themselves. Plus, who am I kidding, I'd fall into depression if someone took my work away from me,* she affirmed to herself, remembering all the birthdays and holidays missed, the relationships strained to their breaking points, and her inability to stop doing what she knew how to do best despite it all.

As she absorbed the serenity of the park, a distant sound of an alert or a siren momentarily pierced the air, a reminder that her world was never too far from crisis. With a resigned sigh, she realized it was time to reconnect. "Come on boy, *vámonos*," she gently instructed her dog, Rocco, who had been relaxing contentedly at her feet, enjoying the cool feel of the grass and the myriad of smells. She clipped his leash, and they began ambling back to the parking lot, her steps reluctant, each one taking her further from peace and closer to the chaos of her work. As she got inside her truck, she saw her phone abandoned on the passenger seat - she intentionally didn't take it with her so she could steal this rare moment of quiet. As the screen lit up, she saw a barrage of notifications—a series of increasingly anxious messages from her partner, Marco, punctuated by missed calls. The first message read simply, "Call me," and as she quickly skimmed through them, the tone of urgency escalated. The last message caught her eye, its words tinged with concern: "It's important. Call me as soon as you see this." With a deep breath, Sofia started the engine and began to drive, immediately dialing Marco and connecting her phone to the truck's speakerphone.

As soon as he picked up, Marco's voice came through, tight with tension. "Where the hell have you been? I've been trying to reach you for hours."

Sofia felt the brief escape evaporating as quickly as it came. "I... I was just taking a short break, Marco. Needed some air. What's going on? What's with the urgency?"

Marco responded, with a mixture of relief and frustration, "The DEA wants to have a meeting. There's been a development on the cartel case; I think they've got something big. They didn't want to say much over the phone, just stressed it was urgent."

"Okay, I'm on my way," Sofia replied, her tone mixing resignation with a spark of her usual determination. Then, trying to lighten the mood, she added, "And here I thought I could sneak away for just a moment without the world falling apart!"

Marco chuckled, his laughter cracking through the line, momentarily easing the tension. "You know the job never sleeps, but hey, we signed up for this, right? I'll see you in ten."

After ending the call with Marco, Sofia's mind raced with the possibilities of what the urgent development might entail. As she drove, her thoughts transitioned from the brief respite of the morning to the pressing realities of her job.

***

As Sofia approached the briefing room, a space encapsulated by glass walls situated at the heart of her office, a wave of discomfort washed over her. She's never liked the transparency of the room, feeling as though it exposed too much to too many eyes. Inside, her team awaited - a mix of anticipation and casual camaraderie in their stances.

Tomás, ever the joker, greeted her with a tease. "Hey, look who finally decided to join us," he said, giving her a playful grin.

"Hey, give her a break. She practically lives here," Javier chimed in with a smile, easing the atmosphere slightly.

"I was just messing around," Tomás quickly added, sensing he might have pushed too far. "Thought she could use a laugh, that's all."

Marco, always keen to keep things on track, didn't miss a beat. "Alright, shall we get started?" he suggested, his voice a grounding force as he gestured towards the large screen dominating one wall.

"Let's do this," Sofia said, her voice firm, mixing determination with readiness as she initiated the video call. The screen flickered to life, connecting her Mexican team with their U.S. counterparts. The room fell silent, tense with anticipation.

Tom Warton, the lead DEA investigator from Berkeley, appeared on the screen, his expression grave. "We've ramped up our surveillance over the past weeks, focusing on anomalous patterns across Berkeley," he began, his tone both urgent and controlled, capturing the full attention of Sofia and her team. "Let's take a look at what we've uncovered."

The first slide showed a series of graphs depicting electricity and water usage over time. Each line graph spiked dramatically, far outstripping the neighborhood's baseline, which was marked in a contrasting color. "These spikes in utility usage at several properties aren't aligning with typical residential patterns. Notice the timing and the magnitude of these spikes—consistent with industrial operations, likely running through the night," He paused, letting the information sink in, then continued. "This pattern of utility usage has flagged these locations as significant points of interest. We believe they could be central to the cartel's activities in the area, coordinating logistics or hiding key assets."

Paul McDowell, from the tactical team, leaned forward. "And the thermal imaging from drones during these spikes—what does it show?"

"Thermal scans indicate significant heat generation from these buildings during off-hours, inconsistent with any normal residential or commercial use," Tom detailed, displaying a thermal image with bright colors indicating heat.

As he switched the slides to aerial photos of the properties marked with data overlays, Sofia's focus sharpened. "Tom, how confident are we that these aren't legitimate businesses operating at unusual hours?" she interjected.

Tom nodded, expecting the query. "Good question, Sofia. We've done our homework—cross-referenced utility accounts with business licenses, conducted stakeouts. There was nothing typical about these activities, and no business licenses match the level of utility use. Plus, informant tips corroborate suspicions of cartel involvement." He added another layer to the map, showing the network of cartel operations stretching from California to Mexico. "Given the cartel's known operational patterns in both California and Mexico, we're looking at a transnational issue. This necessitates a joint operation to effectively dismantle their network across borders."

The next slide detailed the proposed joint operation. "This is our proposed action plan. Synchronized raids, minimal on-ground presence before the strike, and extensive use of drone surveillance to maintain an element of surprise. We need all hands on deck—intelligence, logistics, tactical support."

Michael, one of the senior strategists, voiced a common concern: "What's the risk of tipping off the cartel with our movements?"

As the briefing continued, Sofia absorbed every detail, aware of the stakes. "We need to keep this under the radar—no leaks, no slip-ups. This operation could define our careers and, more importantly, save lives."

Tom concluded, "Exactly. Our success depends on confidentiality and precision. We'll continue updating our intel right up to the hour of the raid."

Sofia took a moment to absorb the intel before responding. "Thanks, Tom. We'll use this as our starting point. Let's get to work on the next steps."

Michael shared a digital map with the group, zooming in on the locations they'd been discussing. "Here are the entry points for each site," he detailed, his cursor hovering over critical spots. "We will need to consider every angle—approach routes, exits, even aerial views for possible drone surveillance."

The tension in the room escalated as Sofia's mind mapped out the operation in real time. She could almost hear the clock ticking down. "We'll need local law enforcement involved from the outset," Sofia said, eyes scanning the team. "They have the additional manpower we need. Also, it's crucial that we leverage the DEA's expertise while ensuring the operation adheres to local jurisdiction and international law. But let's be clear—we're operating off the record. No media, no official channels. This needs to stay under the radar, especially if things go sideways. We can't afford any leaks."

Tom Warton, nodding in acknowledgment, explained, "We've worked closely with your authorities to ensure all legal frameworks are respected. The necessary warrants for the raids have been secured through joint e-fforts, and our SWAT teams are prepared to mobilize," he explained, his expression serious.

The discussion moved seamlessly into operational planning. Sofia's leadership was palpable as she directed the conversation towards logistics.

"This isn't just another tactical raid; we're dismantling a network. We need robust communication lines throughout—encrypted, secure. Marco, you'll manage comms from the command center."

Roy Wayne, the Communications Specialist, nodded, his voice firm. "Our secure command center will handle all communications on our end."

Sofia locked eyes with each of her team members. "Marco, you'll be leading comms from here. Make sure each team has both primary and backup radios. And let's set up encrypted channels on all devices to prevent any interception. Any issues overnight, I'm counting on you to sort them." Sofia then shifted to the technical side. "Aerial surveillance is crucial. Paul, can we get real-time updates from the drones? We need thermal imaging and eyes on the ground before we move in."

"Yes, we've got that covered. We'll have drones equipped with thermal cameras up and running, providing a live feed to the command center," Paul chimed in.

Sofia agreed and then shifted her focus to the team assembly. "Here's the role assignment for the operation," she announced, pulling up a digital roster on the screen. "We have three entry teams. Team one, led by Lieutenant Ramirez, will enter from the north side; team two, under Sergeant Márquez, will cover the south; and I will lead team three and take the west entrance. We'll have snipers in position to cover the exits, and drone operators- you're tasked with giving us eyes in the sky and alerting us to any changes." She then turned to risk management, a solemn edge to her tone. "Now, let's talk risks. We expect minimal civilian presence during the operation, but we've got medical teams and negotiators on standby just in case. We'll also need to account for potential escape routes—make sure your teams are briefed on all possibilities. Any changes, any intel that comes through overnight, we act on it immediately." She stood tall, her voice steady as she finished, "We meet here at 0600. Stay sharp, stay focused, and stay saf e."

With that, the call ended, the screens going dark one by one. Sofia exhaled deeply, a mixture of resolve and exhaustion settling in. Marco lingered by her side as the last screen went black. "You ready for tomorrow?" he asked, his voice quieter now, a touch of concern creeping in.

Sofia exhaled, her gaze sweeping the glass-enclosed room. "I just can't wait for all this to be over," she confessed. She managed a small smile and added, "You know, every time I'm in this room, I feel like I'm in an aquarium, everybody staring at us."

Marco chuckled softly, looking around at the transparent walls as he whispered, "Just imagine they're the ones in the aquarium, not us."

Sofia laughed lightly, her stress easing just a little as she felt a sense of camaraderie with her team. "Right," she replied. "Let's make sure we do this right."

***

Back at a secure compound hidden deep in the outskirts of Tijuana, the Sangre Cartel was busy orchestrating its sprawling network. The warehouse, a scene of organized chaos, was bustling with activity under the harsh glow of bare bulbs. Individuals measured, weighed, and sealed various substances, while others managed detailed ledgers, documenting the transactions. The ambiance was markedly different; the air hung heavy with the scent of tobacco and a palpable tension that seemed to permeate the walls. Local reggaeton and salsa tunes were playing from a small speaker, adding a splash of color to a very gray and serious scene. The compound buzzed with the low murmur of conversations as members of the cartel, rough-and-ready types known more for action than strategy, adorned with tattoos that told tales of loyalty and violence, busied themselves by loading trucks with contraband, preparing for a night run to California. They worked with a sense of urgency yet, in contrast with Sofia's station - without any formal coordination. Men smoked casually, the cigarettes hanging from their lips as they hefted boxes into the vehicles. Nearby, Vargas' men stood watch with a confident, intimidating stance at every exit. Their eyes were vigilant, hands never straying far from the guns holstered at their sides, ensuring no unwanted disruptions to the night's operations.

In contrast to the rough exteriors of the loaders, a solitary figure by a makeshift desk seemed out of place, yet was a vital piece to the operation. Wearing a tank top, he was surrounded by monitors and radios, his appearance less intimidating but marked by an intensity of focus. His demeanor hinted at a past possibly spent on the other side of the law—a hint of an undercover agent still lingering despite his current allegiance to the cartel. His role was clear: to provide the intelligence that kept their operations one step ahead of law enforcement, ensuring the night's plans would proceed without interference. Joining the cartel out of a deep-seated greed and a desire for power, Daniel Cortez leveraged his tech expertise to rise up in ranks and become the boss' right hand, carefully covering all phone calls and cartel communications to keep them unnoticed by the police and maintain a low profile.

Suspicions were born out of the recent fires where they lost Gustavo Calo's family, many crew members and Vargas' own cousin - there was a clear pattern, and it was only a matter of time before they could figure out who was moving against them and eliminate him. They must have inside information, Vargas thought, so he instructed Cortez to do a check of their team's outgoing communications right before each operation. With a few clicks, he was deep into the encrypted communications of the cartel members, his eyes scanning for anomalies, when suddenly, he paused. Daniel's face darkened as he stumbled upon something alarming—a series of encrypted texts on the phone of one of their own, known only by the code name "Maverick." These messages were to an unknown number, and they were consistently sent about 24 hours before the mysterious fires at their safe houses, was too coincidental to ignore. The gravity of his discovery was not lost on him. Without alerting anyone around him, Cortez made his way through the dimly lit room towards the cartel's leader. He leaned in close, his voice barely a whisper, his expression grave. "Boss, I think we have a mole. Maverick has been sending encrypted messages just before each incident at our facilities."

At the head of the table stood the elusive figure known only as "El Patrón," a man whose real name few dared to utter. His presence commanded attention, and his eyes, sharp and calculating, missed nothing. El Patrón's reaction was swift and fierce. His hand slammed down on the nearby desk, making everyone in the room flinch—the sound echoing off the walls, mirroring the sudden surge of anger in his eyes. He seized Cortez by the shirt, pulling him close. His grip was iron-tight, his face just inches away from Daniel's. "Find him now!" he barked, his voice a menacing growl. After a tense moment, he released him and swiftly turned his attention to the operational map spread out on the table. "We need to adjust the routes," he declared with a calm but authoritative tone, pointing at the lines that marked their current smuggling paths. "The heat is on, and the gringos are getting smarter."

As he scanned the room, his gaze settling on each of his men in turn, he added, "If Maverick is our leak, we'll flush him out and get everything he knows." The stakes were high and the success of their upcoming operation was critical. Everyone knew it, and the tension was thick as a smoke, spreading fear and filling everyone with adrenaline. "Prepare to move out," he commanded abruptly. "Take everything. You know the drill, boys. No trails, no traces." His eyes then fixed back on Daniel, who was straightening his shirt, still rattled. "And Cortez, keep your ears open and your tech tricks handy. Anyone talks, they won't see the sunrise."

Once El Patrón's mind was made, there was no going back. The cartel was not just a criminal organization; it was a well-oiled machine, quick to adapt and react. As the guys were finishing loading in the background, Cortez swiftly set up a meet at the docks, intended as a trap for Maverick. "Find out who he's working with. Make it look routine," the boss instructed his men. He then fixed his eyes on Toro, his tone dropping to a menacing whisper. "You know what to do."

The man, known simply as Toro due to his massive build and intimidating presence, caught his gaze and cracked his knuckles, an ominous grin spreading across his face. "Señor" he nodded in confirmation. His reputation for extracting information was well-known within the cartel, and his methods were as effective as they were brutal. With a nod, he moved towards the preparations, ready to play his part in the trap for Maverick, ensuring that by the time the night was over, they would know exactly who the mole was working with.

The compound, nestled deep in the outskirts of Tijuana, hummed with the low murmur of activity as the cartel moved to erase any traces of their presence. Under the cover of darkness, the trucks rolled out, each movement precise and unhurried, but laden with the tension of what was to come. El Patrón stood in the shadows, his figure almost blending into the night. His orders were clear, his voice a low murmur barely audible over the sound of engines. "Everything must go smoothly. We can't afford any mistakes—not tonight." His gaze lingered on the horizon, where the city lights of Tijuana met the dark sky, a stark reminder of the empire he had raised from the shadows.

***

Jack's phone buzzed quietly against the wooden nightstand, the screen lighting up the dim bedroom with a message from an unknown number. He squinted at the message that flashed across the screen: "Urgent - got some information. Meet me at our usual spot, ASAP." He knew immediately who it was. The brevity of the message, paired with its suddenness, sent a ripple of alarm through Jack. He grabbed his keys and headed out, the uneasy feeling settling deep in his gut.

As he drove through the quiet streets towards the address, Jack's mind raced with possibilities. What had he uncovered that couldn't wait until morning? His grip tightened on the steering wheel as he turned down the familiar street, only to find the door of the apartment ajar, the frame splintered as if forced open. He slowed down, turning off his headlights to not draw any attention, and parked a few house numbers away. This didn't look promising, and someone could be watching.

Jack sneaked inside cautiously, where the chaos was palpable- the place had been ransacked. Papers were strewn about, drawers yanked open, and contents spilled like the aftermath of a storm. The furniture was displaced, some of it broken, all unmistakable signs of a struggle or a frantic search. Jack paused at the threshold, his eyes quickly taking in the scene of disarray. *What did you get yourself into?* He wondered.

Jack moved cautiously, his senses heightened, scanning for any sign of Maverick or clues to what might have happened. A sudden noise caught his attention as he stepped over a scattered pile of photographs. He rushed to the window just in time to see the taillights of a black SUV disappearing around the corner, its presence more a shadow than a solid form in the dim light. The screech of tires on asphalt echoed in the otherwise silent night, and a bitter realization hit Jack that he was possibly just moments too late.

Maverick was Jack's inside man for the cartel. He was a fellow in his 40s who emigrated from Mexico illegally when he was only 5 years old. He knew how to blend in anywhere, which earned him the nickname "The Chameleon". Him missing was a big red flag for Jack - and seeing the black SUV confirmed his suspicions that the cartel finally figured out he played the double-agent role.

With his contact missing and the situation more dangerous than ever, Jack's instincts kicked in. He couldn't afford to waste a second - he trusted that Maverick knows better than to talk, but that could cost him his life. Racing back to his car, he fired up the engine and peeled out after the fading tail lights of the black SUV, keeping his headlights off to not raise any suspicion - he had to stay invisible, or he might lose the chance of getting closer to the cartel's hideout. Every second mattered, and the high stakes only sharpened his focus as he navigated through the dark streets, determined to catch up to the vehicle that might lead him to Maverick and deeper into the treacherous web of the cartel. "This might work out better than I thought," Jack whispered to himself, now hopeful that he might save his friend but also get the chance to encounter his sworn enemy – Vargas.

Jack's pursuit led him to the Oakland port—a predictable location for a cartel that frequently smuggled goods. "Of course," he muttered to himself, his voice barely audible over the hum of his car's engine as he eased the vehicle into a shadowed spot between other cars, nestled under the cover of surrounding trees. From his vantage point, he had a clear view of the warehouse.

In the distance, he could make out the figures of thugs, unmistakably rough in their handling of a hooded figure who was being shoved around the dock. That had to be Maverick, Jack surmised, recognizing the posture of a man whose hands were bound and who seemed to be playing dumb. His muffled protests of "What the hell is going on?" carrying faintly across the water.

Jack scanned the area meticulously, noting each exit from the warehouse and counting the guards he could see patrolling the perimeter. His mind raced as he pieced together a plan on the spot, calculating the risks of a direct confrontation against the need to rescue Maverick before it was too late.

"Nothing I haven't dealt with before," he whispered to himself, the familiar adrenaline of the chase settling into his veins. He smirked slightly, despite the danger, adding under his breath, "It should be a walk in the park. Hang in there, Maverick."

As Jack approached the Port, he sensed the chill of the evening sea breeze mingled with the acrid tang of salt and diesel; the sensation running all the way down his neck. Oakland Port, usually a bustling hub during the day, now lay eerily silent under the cloak of night. Sparse lighting from old, weather-beaten lampposts cast long shadows, distorting the shapes of moored boats and distant warehouses into looming specters. The rhythmic lapping of the waves against the docks played a haunting melody, punctuated occasionally by the distant shout or the clang of metal from somewhere deep within the maze of containers and equipment. The smell of the ocean was overpowering, filled with the promise of mystery and danger.

Before entering, Jack paused in the shadows, taking a moment to assess the situation. He sent a message to someone that read, "I am at the OP. Shit could go down. Might need backup. They've got our Chameleon." Almost immediately, his phone vibrated with a reply, "Don't do anything stupid. Wait for me."

But as Jack stowed his phone, a distant scream cut through the night, slicing through the ambient sounds of the waterfront. The scream was muffled, desperate, coming from the direction of the warehouses. Despite the clear warning, Jack's instinct urged him to act. With only a second to make the call, he chose a middle ground; he couldn't just wait while his friend might be in danger, but he also didn't want to barge in unprepared. *Here goes nothing.*

His infiltration of the warehouse was as silent as it was deadly. As he moved through the labyrinthine warehouse, he tried to justify his recklessness in his mind; *Just a quick look around. That's all this needs to be.* Each shadow cast by the flickering overhead lights felt like a potential threat, each distant echo a possible alarm. *Stay sharp, keep it quiet,* he reminded himself, tightening his grip on whatever makeshift weapon he had found outside, the muffled screams guiding him to the grim scene. He navigated crates and steel shelving, his footsteps deliberate and soundless. He paused, crouched behind a stack of crates, and surveyed the next corridor. The guards were sporadic but predictable, their rounds lazy and lackluster. *Amateurs*, he scoffed internally, but even amateurs were dangerous when cornered.

The first guard was stationed near a stack of wooden crates, his back turned to the approaching danger. Jack moved like a shadow, silent and swift. Before the man could react, the pipe came down hard on the back of his skull with a sickening thud. The guard collapsed in a heap, and Jack caught him before he hit the ground, lowering the limp body with practiced ease. He quickly secured the man's wrists and ankles with the rope he carried, gagging him with a piece of torn fabric from the man's own shirt. Jack wiped his hands on his pants, his face expressionless. It wasn't personal—it never was. Deeper into the warehouse, he found two more guards. They were chatting casually, their voices low but distinct in the stillness. Jack crouched behind a stack of pallets, assessing the situation. Two against one wasn't ideal, but Jack had long since learned how to turn the odds in his favor. He picked up a loose metal bolt from the floor and threw it toward the opposite side of the room. The sharp *clink* against the concrete echoed, drawing the guards' attention. As they moved to investigate, Jack struck. The first man didn't have time to scream. Jack's arm wrapped around his neck in a vice-like grip, the Swiss knife in his other hand slicing clean and deep across his carotid artery. The guard's body sagged as Jack lowered him to the ground, the pooling blood glinting darkly in the dim light. The second man turned just in time to see his partner fall. His hand reached for his weapon, but Jack was faster. A quick, brutal swing of the pipe struck his temple, sending him sprawling. Jack pounced, the knife flashing again as he ensured there would be no recovery. Breathing heavily, Jack stood over the bodies, his mind cold and focused. He wiped the knife on the guard's jacket, his eyes scanning the area for any sign of movement. The silence that followed was deafening.

This is what it takes, Jack reminded himself, though the words felt hollow. Each life he took was a necessary step toward dismantling Vargas' empire, but the weight of his actions never left him. The brutality he employed wasn't born from cruelty, but from necessity—and from the dark corners of his own pain. He moved further into the warehouse, his senses heightened, every nerve on edge. The faint sound of muffled screams grew louder, drawing him toward the grim scene he had come to investigate. Jack adjusted his grip on the knife, his jaw set in grim determination. *No one walks away from this,* he muttered under his breath. As he neutralized another unsuspecting guard with a swift, silent motion, a surge of adrenaline sharpened his focus. *Focus on the mission. Find Maverick. Get out. No heroics.* Yet, as he edged closer to the source of the screams, his resolve was tested. The reality of the cruelty within these walls pressed in on him, igniting a spark of anger. *These people pay for their savagery today,* his thoughts a dark promise to the shadows. He pressed on, the screams now clearer, more desperate. *I'm coming, hold on,* he projected silently with a tinge of desperation, hoping somehow his resolve could change the outcome of what was surely a horrific scene ahead.

He identified a strategic spot where supplies, likely flammable, were stored. His plan was simple: start a small fire there, enough to trigger the fire alarms without causing widespread damage. This would create chaos, pulling the guards from their posts. Silently, Jack made his way to the location. He used a cloth and whatever he could find that would ignite and reach the smoke detectors swiftly. Pulling out his zippo lighter, he flicked it open, striking a spark. He stared at the flame for a moment, in awe of how something small can cause a damage so big, even take and destroy lives. *No time to dwell on it.* The flame caught quickly, more aggressive than anticipated. Jack retreated swiftly, merging back into the shadows. The first wail of the alarm cut through the air, shrill and demanding. Panic ensued among the guards as they scrambled to address the emergency, their focus shifting from guarding to evacuation protocols.

"Go and check that out, and don't be long," the guard barked at another, who hurried out of the room.

The diversion was working; the guards were distracted, giving him the critical window he needed. Seizing the moment, Jack incapacitated the remaining guard with a swift, silent takedown. He throws in a smoke bomb to incapacitate El Toro. The room was a tableau of cruelty; Maverick was barely conscious, slumped against a wall. The air was thick with the stench of blood and fear. He saw that a few of his fingernails had been removed, each missing nail a testament to the brutal interrogation he had endured. He quickly untied Maverick, whispering urgently, "We need to move. Now."

As the confrontation escalated, Jack found himself not just fighting to save a life, but caught in a trap that could cost him his own.

As they neared one of the exits, a door slammed open. A shadowed figure raised a gun and fired a shot towards them. Time was moving slower than ever. Jack reacted instinctively, dodging the bullet, which, to his horror, found its mark in Maverick instead. For a moment, Jack's composure cracked as panic set in. He caught Maverick as he fell, dragging him towards cover, and turned around to deliver a fatal shot to the thug's head. "Damn it," Jack muttered as he looked at Maverick's wound - his rage now overcome with fear for his informer's life. They barely made it a few yards outside the warehouse when the roar of an explosion suddenly tore the air. Fire erupted from one side of the building, casting a ferocious light over the scene. The shock of the blast gave Jack the opportunity he needed. "Keep moving!" Jack shouted over the sound of crumbling walls and alarms blaring into the night.

"There they are!" one of the thugs yelled, and gunfire followed.

He half-carried, half-dragged Maverick, whose strength was failing. The fire illuminated their escape, casting long, erratic shadows as they stumbled over debris. "Come on, man, hold it together. We've been through worse, haven't we?" Jack pleaded, his voice a mix of command and desperation. Maverick, struggling for breath, managed a weak smile.

"It's okay, Jack... you tried," he gasped, his voice fading.

"Stay with me... you gotta stay awake!"Jack urged, pulling him closer. Suddenly, he felt a crushing blow to the back of his head. In the chaos, one of the thugs had managed to sneak up behind them. The impact sent Jack reeling forward, his grip on Maverick loosening. As he staggered, his lighter fell from his pocket, clattering on the concrete—the J&J letters softly illuminated by the moonlight. The world spun violently around him, and as his knees hit the ground, darkness claimed him.

In that darkness, a vivid memory flashed before his eyes, as tangible as if he were living it in that moment. He is back on that sunlit hilltop, the sky impossibly blue above them. He and Jen are lying on a blanket after a long hike, the grass dotted with wildflowers; the world spread out below them like a patchwork quilt. Little toddler Ellie is scampering about, her laughter ringing clear as she brings them leaves, each one a treasure. They are cuddling close, the warmth of the sun mingling with the soft caress of the breeze, the moment suspended in a dreamy, golden haze.

When consciousness returned, it brought with it the harsh reality of cold metal against his wrists and the looming figure of Mateo Vargas. The room was sparse, illuminated by a single bulb that swung gently above his head, casting erratic shadows. The smell of blood from the tortures Maverick endured was still in the air. Vargas watched him with a predatory gaze, the glow of a cigar in between his lips making Jack despise him even more.

"So you are the one who's been causing all the trouble," Vargas sneered, as the echoes of an unfinished conflict hung heavy in the air. The room buzzed with the tension of unspoken threats, his thugs milling about, ready for a command.

One thug leaned close to another, a smirk playing on his lips as he whispered just loud enough for Jack to hear, "Think he'll last longer than the last one?" - he asked, patting a wooden baton in his left hand.

"What do we have, eh? A gringo? Do you know what we do to gringos when they show up without an invitation?" another thug joked, eliciting a coarse laugh from his companions.

The room filled with the low, menacing laughter of men too accustomed to power and cruelty.

"The question is, what do we do to gringos who attack the family of Mateo Vargas," added the boss himself, gritting his teeth with anger and the desire for revenge. *Can there even be "justice" when he started cheating the game from the start?* Vargas motioned to his men, who stepped forward, each blow they delivered calculated to intimidate without impairing Jack's ability to speak.

Despite the pain, Jack's resolve hardened; he gritted his teeth, determined not to give them anything. "I am not a cop. I work alone," Jack kept muttering, each word punctuated by a grunt as another fist connected.

Vargas watched for a moment before stepping in himself, his fists adding to the brutality of the interrogation. "This lone wolf act won't save you here," he taunted, his frustration mounting with Jack's steadfast silence. He leaned in close, his voice low and menacing. "Names. Affiliations. Speak, or it gets much worse. What the hell are you doing here, and how did you find us?"

Jack didn't budge. Despite the pain, he started laughing uncontrollably. "I have been on to you, Vargas. You don't even know how long..." Jack muttered, struggling to speak, yet his face was showing signs of joy.

Matteo Vargas raised an eyebrow, struggling to remember who this guy was, and started chuckling too, his laughter sounding more like crackling that could send shivers down anyone's spine. "Wait, I know who you are. You are the guy who survived the shooting. I thought you were dead. Last I heard, your car was unrecognizable on that day" - he looked at one of his men, trying to figure out if they lied to him.

The thug's confident posture suddenly went into full submission. "I swear, jefe, I saw photos with my own eyes."

Suddenly, the distant wail of sirens cut through the tense air and brought the cartel's amusement to an abrupt end. Vargas paused, signaling his men with a sharp gesture. "Wrap this up, our business here is done," he ordered, ready to disappear into the night.

"But boss, he hasn't told us anything," one of his underlings protested with desperation in his tone.

Vargas stopped, his silhouette outlined against the dim light. "It doesn't matter. He's seen too much. Make sure he disappears, this time for good," he replied coldly, his command final.

The thugs moved quickly, adding weights to Jack's legs. They dragged him towards the dock, his body battered and barely conscious. Just as they were about to throw him into the murky waters, headlights pierced the darkness, and a car skidded to a halt. A shadowy figure stepped out, moving with trained precision that belied the urgency of the situation. The dock, previously poorly lit by intermittent pools of light from old, flickering lamps, was now dramatically illuminated by the glow of the fire that Jack started. The additional light threw long, dancing shadows, adding a layer of uncertainty and chaos as the area shifted between light and dark. Gunfire erupted almost immediately as he approached, but he was prepared. Bullets ricocheted off the metal containers with sharp pings, creating a chaotic symphony of noise and danger. He ducked behind a shipping container, the cold metal a brief respite, as he assessed the situation. Peering around the corner, he saw two of Vargas's men advancing. He waited, breath held, timing his movements with their sporadic bursts of fire. As they reloaded, he sprang from cover, closing the distance with swift strides. The first thug barely had time to raise his weapon before a well-placed punch knocked the gun away, sending it skittering across the concrete. A quick elbow to the jaw knocked the thug out cold. The second, alerted by the noise, turned just in time to see his companion fall. He swung wildly with his gun, a desperate club, but the rescuer deflected the blow with his arm, feeling the jarring impact radiate up his forearm. With a practiced maneuver, he twisted the gun out of the thug's grasp and used his momentum to throw him into the side of the container. The thug slumped down, stunned and disoriented.

The sirens grew louder, an urgent reminder of the encroaching law enforcement. The local police, already mobilized and on high alert from assisting with the day's coordinated raids alongside Sofia's team and the DEA, were closing in on this new location.

Breathing heavily, he scanned quickly for more threats—two more closing in, one trying to flank him. He had to get to Jack before they did. Suddenly, a bullet grazed his side, a sharp reminder of his vulnerability. He ducked back, using the container for cover, and fired twice with the stolen gun. The first shot missed, whizzing past into the dark water beyond, but the second caught one thug in the shoulder, sending him sprawling. Panting, he didn't pause to rest. Every second mattered. He sprinted towards the edge of the dock, where he spotted Jack being manhandled towards the edge, his captors busily attaching weights to his legs. Shouts filled the air as they prepared to dispose of him in the murky waters below. As he fired his handgun, keeping the attackers at a distance, he grabbed Jack, pulling him back from the edge. A bullet hits the weights right next to his foot. The impact sent the weights clattering across the concrete, buying precious seconds. "Hang on, we're almost clear!" he yelled over the gunfire, his voice strained with urgency. Bullets whizzed past, sparking off the metal containers as they made a desperate dash for the car parked in the shadows

Just then, the night erupted into further chaos as Sofia's team, as well as the DEA, stormed the marina. Each team moved in from their designated directions: north, south, and west, as meticulously planned. Lights from police vehicles flashed rhythmically, cutting through the darkness and illuminating the dock with stark, sweeping beams. The sound of boots on the ground was almost drowned out by the roar of helicopters overhead, their searchlights piercing the smoke and shadows created by the ongoing fire. "Police! Drop your weapons!" The commands echoed over the chaos, yet the cartel members were quick to return fire, leading to a fierce shootout.

The precision of their approach, dictated by the digital maps and aerial surveillance data shared during the briefing, allowed them to encircle the area efficiently, leaving little room for the cartel members to maneuver. The teams, communicating through encrypted channels led by Marco from the command center, coordinated their advances and containment strategies seamlessly, ensuring each member was accounted for and each threat assessed.

But then, for a split second, everything started to go wrong. In the confusion, Vargas seized the opportunity to target the law enforcement officers, firing multiple shots. Sofia, leading her team towards the critical point of the raid, was caught off guard. Bullets struck, the impacts absorbed by her bulletproof vest, yet knocking her down, and one grazing her shoulder, sending a searing pain through her arm.

Jack, now more alert due to the adrenaline, noticed the injured officer in the line of fire and made a split-second decision. Ignoring the shouts of his rescuer—"Jack, what are you doing? We need to go!"—yet he dashed towards Sofia, determined to help her despite the pain he was in. Ducking bullets, he reached her side, pulling her to safety behind a large shipping container.

"Stay down!" he instructed, assessing her injuries quickly. Despite her confusion and pain, Sofia managed a nod, her training keeping her alert. "Did he get you?" he asks.

"It's just a scratch."

"Apply pressure. You'll be safe back here, at least for a little while."

Despite the tight encirclement by the DEA teams, the situation rapidly devolved into chaos when Vargas, ever cunning and desperate, saw a fleeting opportunity in the thick of gunfire. As the SWAT team advanced, their focus momentarily divided between apprehending cartel members and responding to the heavy exchange of fire, Vargas and Cortez acted. Daniel, leveraging his intimate knowledge of the dock's layout—a result of his role in planning escape routes and contingencies—signaled to Vargas. They made a dash for a previously camouflaged exit point, barely noticeable and not visible to aerial surveillance due to its cover under a makeshift lean-to stacked with fishing nets and barrels.

Jack, ensuring Sofia was no longer in immediate danger and using the fact that the police were occupied with Vargas to make a clean exit, reluctantly followed his rescuer back to the car. They sped away just as the police secured the area. The night air whipped through the open windows, with the sounds of pursuit fading behind them, replaced by the ragged breaths of two men who'd narrowly escaped death.

Jack, battered and bruised, managed to mutter, "About time you showed up", his voice raw with both pain and gratitude.

The mysterious rescuer merely offered a grim smile, "Next time, try not to get killed, Jack," he replied, driving them both into the safety of the night, leaving behind the sound of sirens blending with the ocean's roar.

As Sofia's team reeled from the unexpected barrage, Vargas and Daniel slipped through this narrow passageway. The roar of a waiting speedboat's engine broke through the sound of the firefight as they fired back, not aiming to hit but to create enough suppression to cover their escape. They jumped aboard, with Daniel kicking off the dock as Vargas fired one last round towards a nearby transformer. The resulting explosion wasn't large, but it was enough to create a brief, blinding light, further disorienting the law enforcement officers and providing the crucial seconds they needed. As the police closed in on the warehouse, the cartel's resistance began to falter, their numbers dwindling under the coordinated assault. The SWAT teams regrouped, rapidly assessing their options. Marco, active from the unified command center, relayed new orders, directing the aerial units to track the escapees while ground units secured the area and attended to the injured, including Sofia. In the chaos, Jack and his rescuer made it without putting a target on their back.

***

They soon entered an apartment that was filled with a tense silence, broken only by the soft clinks of medical supplies as Xavier treats Jack's wounds. The room was sparsely lit, shadows cast by the dim light adding to the somber atmosphere. There's a sense of temporary safety, punctuated by the sharp, antiseptic smell. The muffled sounds of the city at night filter through a slightly open window, a reminder of the world continuing outside their immediate crisis.

Xavier works with efficient, practiced motions, but there's an edge to his actions, a tightness in his jaw that speaks volumes. "You should've waited, Jack," Xavier mutters, his voice tight with restrained frustration. His hands are steady, but his brow is furrowed, reflecting a mix of concern and irritation. The tension in the room escalates as he continues. "You know how risky it was to go in alone. We've discussed this."

Jack sits shirtless on the couch, wincing slightly as Xavier patches him up, the pain from his wounds secondary to the weight of Xavier's words. He looks weary but alert, his mind clearly on other things. He's used to acting on instinct, but Xavier's rebuke hits hard, reminding him of the stakes—not just for him, but for everyone involved. Jack's response is quiet, reflective of his understanding but also his innate drive to act when danger looms. "I had to move," he finally says, his voice low. "There wasn't time."

Xavier pauses in his ministrations, looking squarely at Jack. His expression softens slightly, the earlier sharpness giving way to reluctant understanding. Yet, he shakes his head, his next words laced with a stern caution. "And if you had been compromised, Jack? What then? We're in this together, you can't just—"

The conversation was sparse, filled with long pauses as both men processed the night's events and their implications. Jack broke one such silence with a low, urgent question. "Did you make sure we weren't followed?" His voice was low, almost a whisper, as if he was afraid of being overheard.

Xavier paused, gave Jack a flat look, and responded dryly, "What do you think, Jack? This is not my first day on the job." His tone is a mix of sarcasm and reassurance, trying to inject a slight humor into the gravity of their situation.

Their intense conversation was interrupted by a soft buzzing from Jack's phone, lying on the small, cluttered table beside them. Ellie. Xavier sighed, a long and weary sound, as he finished bandaging Jack. "You look like hell," he remarked, eyeing the deep gash along Jack's brow and the swelling that had turned his left eye into a dark, puffy slit. "What are you going to tell her?" he asked, changing the subject to something equally important but less confrontational.

Jack rubbed a hand over his face, feeling the stubble and the weight of his decisions. His expression, marred by bruises that streaked down his jawline like watercolors on a rough canvas, shifted—a mix of pain and resolve playing across his features. "Well, I am a firefighter, shit happens," he attempted to joke, but the humor didn't quite reach his eyes.

Xavier chuckled humorlessly, "You think she'll buy that? She ain't a kid anymore, Jack. You have got to be more careful."

His words hit as a heavy reminder of the risks he took, not just for himself, but for those he cared about. No one really knew which was the right and the wrong answer.

***

As the last echoes of gunfire died down, the scene at Oakland Harbor transformed into a methodical gathering of evidence. Police officers and agents alike moved through the chaos with practiced efficiency, securing handcuffed cartel members. "We got a few of them," Javier announced, his voice a mix of relief and resolve.

"Forget it. They ain't going to give us anything," added Tom Warton, a seasoned DEA agent, as he watched the suspects being led away. His statement hung in the air, a stark reminder of the tough road ahead in extracting information. While they might have uncovered part of an operation and held a few of them in custody, this was running way deeper than that, his experience told him. They needed the brain behind the operation. Not the people who were replaceable.

Meanwhile, the glow of emergency lights reflected off the water, and the rhythmic hiss of water hoses echoed faintly in the distance. The firefighters from the Berkeley Fire Department were also on scene - dispatched as part of a mutual aid request from Oakland Fire Department due to the scale of the emergency. Among them was Abe. He hadn't been scheduled for this shift—called in at the last minute to replace a colleague from B shift. As he packed away the hoses, his thoughts drifted. *Always B shift letting the side down,* he mused internally, shaking his head with a hint of humor in his silent critique - *This shit rarely happens when Jack and I are on shift.* His gaze kept shifting back to the police activity, the thought of Jack making him recall the conversation they had at the Old Brewery about the harbor and how there is more than what meets the eye. *Maybe that bastard is onto something,* he thought to himself, a newfound suspicion creeping into his thoughts.

Meanwhile, Sofia, slightly bruised but determined, sat on the edge of an open ambulance. Medics fussed around her, but she brushed off their concerns with a persistent, "I'm fine." Her eyes scanned the area, the adrenaline still coursing through her veins. "We need to go back out there. They must be close," she kept insisting.

Abe, wrapping up his duties, approached a police officer to inquire about the cause of the fire for his report. "Do you have any leads yet?" he asked, his tone professional yet curious.

The officer nodded towards the evidence bag being sealed by a crime scene technician. "It was certainly an intentional fire. Whatever happened inside must have triggered it. Not much evidence to how it started, but it spread from over there," - he pointed at the section that Jack lit up. "Oh, and I found this outside. We don't know if it means anything yet, but it could've been used to start the fire," he said, holding up a bag containing a lighter.

Abe's gaze fixed on the item, a flicker of recognition washing over his face. "Can I see that for a moment?" he asked the officer, his voice barely a murmur, betraying a tremor of anxiety. Heart sinking, he reached out, his fingers tracing the letters through the plastic, his pulse quickening with each realization. It was a lighter he had seen a million times, unmistakable with its etched initials 'J&J'—*Jack & Jen.*

It means everything... he thought as he tightened his grip around the bag, the implications of this discovery sending a chill down his spine. "Jack...what did you get yourself into?" he whispered under his breath, the weight of the moment settling in. The familiar object, now a key piece of evidence, linked his friend to the chaos of the night. Torn between duty and loyalty, Abe felt the edges of his world blur as he grappled with the next steps, knowing that whatever came next could alter their lives forever. He thanked the officer and walked back to the fire truck, without saying another word; his demeanor - grave.

PART 2: FLAMES OF DECEPTION

Chapter 6

1981

It was the height of summer in 1981 when Jack Singer's life took an unexpected turn. The sun blazed down on the sparkling water, its rays bouncing off the waves like shards of glass. Jack strode toward the small diving school by the marina, his heartbeat quickening with anticipation. He was just 22, fresh- faced and full of restless energy, eager to chase the thrill of adventure wherever he could find it. And learning how to scuba dive was the next feat on his list.

The diving school Jack walked into that fateful summer was a modest operation tucked away in a quiet corner of the marina, its weathered sign simply reading "East Bay Diving Academy." The building itself was unassuming—whitewashed walls speckled with sun-worn paint and a row of oxygen tanks leaning haphazardly against one side. Despite its appearance, the school carried an air of purpose and quiet pride, promising more than what meets the eye. Several of Jack's uni friends vouched for it, and they were local, so they knew this place has been here long enough.

Inside, the academy offered an intimate and hands-on approach to training, specializing in small groups and personalized instruction. The curriculum was tailored not only to teach the technical skills of scuba diving but also to prepare students for the unpredictable challenges of Northern

California's often temperamental waters. Safety was paramount, and the instructors instilled a deep respect for the ocean's power, focusing on risk management and watermanship techniques that set their students apart.

"Jack Singer?" a deep voice called from the shade of the building.

Jack turned to see his instructor for the first time: Xavier Graves. Tall and athletic, with a sun-weathered face and sharp, calculating eyes, Xavier had an undeniable and slightly intimidating presence. There was something about the way he carried himself—calm yet commanding, with an undercurrent of intensity—that immediately drew Jack's attention. This guy doesn't look like a scuba instructor, he thought to himself. "Yeah, that's me," Jack said, offering a handshake.

Xavier's grip was firm, his expression unreadable. "You ever been underwater before, Jack?"

"Not like this," Jack admitted.

"Well," Xavier said with a faint smirk, "let's see if you've got what it takes to handle what's down there."

Xavier had a knack for turning novices into confident, capable divers. His teaching style and excellent leadership was equal parts rigorous and inspiring, pushing students to their limits while fostering a deep appreciation for the underwater world. He believed that diving was not just a skill but a mindset—one that required focus, discipline, and the ability to stay calm under pressure.

For Jack, the school felt like more than a place to learn—it was a gateway to something bigger, something that would soon alter the course of his life forever. From the moment he stepped into the academy, he felt a pull, a sense that this unassuming place held the key to a destiny he hadn't yet imagined.

As Xavier's sharp eyes appraised Jack's raw potential, it quickly became clear to him that he was more than a young man eager to explore the ocean. He saw potential inside Singer that even he couldn't realize himself. "Could this be the hidden gem..." Xavier thought. The spark in Jack—a thirst for challenge, a willingness to push boundaries, was there as a clear sign to move forward. And so, with every dive, every lesson, and every piece of advice that stretched beyond the basics, Xavier began to mold Jack into something more than just a skilled diver.

As the weeks went by, their sessions became less about diving and more about the unspoken lessons Xavier wove into their conversations. "You've got potential, Jack," Xavier said one afternoon as they loaded tanks onto the boat. "Not just for this, but for something bigger. You ever thought about using your skills for something... important?"

Jack frowned, wiping sweat from his brow. "What do you mean?"

Xavier leaned against the railing, his gaze fixed on the horizon. "You like responsibility. You've got guts. And you don't panic, you think, and you just go for it. You've got that fire in you—the one that makes people like us restless. 7ere's a way to use that, if you're willing to learn." It started small—physical drills, mental exercises, and strategy games that seemed like harmless fun at first. But soon, Jack realized Xavier was teaching him more than just diving. He was preparing him for something far more dangerous.

On one of his next scuba diving lessons, Xavier cancelled the class for everyone else but Jack. "Where is everyone else?" Jack asked, looking around, wondering if he turned up on the wrong day or something. Xavier turned to face him fully, his expression unreadable. "It's just you and me today. Let's go for a ride to some of the local dive areas. You will be surprised what the San Francisco Bay hides beneath its murky surface."

He pointed at the boat, its white hull gleaming in the early morning light, ready to embrace the endless mystery of the ocean beyond the docks. The scent of salt and diesel hung in the crisp air, mixing with the quiet hum of the harbor as seagulls circled overhead. Jack hesitantly followed Xavier aboard, the wooden deck creaking beneath his feet like a whisper of secrets waiting to be uncovered. He had a sense that he was about to uncover one t oday.

They were bracing the waters, the salty breeze gently washing over their faces. Suddenly, Xavier stopped the boat and joined Jack, who was bathing in the warm sun on the deck, caught in one of his moments of peace and tranquility that the ocean's blues were so good at providing. "Jack, I want to offer you a chance to do something bigger. To protect people, to make a difference. But it's not easy, and it's not always safe. I'm going to go straight to the point. I'm talking about covert operations—joining the CIA."

Jack blinked, taken aback. "The CIA? You're serious?"

"Dead serious," Xavier replied. "It's dangerous, Jack. You'll have to be someone else, someone who lives in the shadows while keeping your life looking normal on the surface. If you take this on, you'll need to swear to secrecy. That means not involving anyone—not your friends, not your family, and especially not your wife."

The mention of Jen made Jack hesitate. "I... I don't know if I can keep something like this from her. She's everything to me."

Xavier's expression softened, but only slightly. "I get it. But the moment you involve her, you put her at risk. And I'm not just talking about her safety—I'm talking about what this kind of life does to people. Secrets like this don't just weigh on you. They weigh on everyone you love, whether they know it or not."

Jack stared at the deck, his mind racing with hundreds of questions, his feelings a bitter-sweet mix of excitement and worry. "And what happens to my life? My career? I can't just disappear into some secret job."

"You won't," Xavier said. "That's the whole point. You keep your day job. Something flexible, something that lets you travel without raising suspicion. Your life stays intact, on the surface at least. But when you're called in, you go. No questions, no excuses."

Jack let out a breath, the enormity of the offer sinking in. He still struggled to comprehend the seriousness and depth of Xavier's proposal. "Why me?"

Xavier smiled faintly, running his fingers through his hair. "Because I see in you what I saw in myself when I started. You've got the courage to face danger head-on, the brains to think your way out of tough situations, and the heart to do what's right—no matter the cost."

Jack looked out at the ocean, the waves crashing against the hull of the boat. Part of him wanted to walk away, to say no, and return to the life he knew. But another part, the part that had always craved purpose and challenge, felt a spark of curiosity and a pull toward something greater. He could make a difference and have the thrill that he always sought. He doesn't really need to give up his life or his future career. "Alright," Jack said finally, his voice steady. "What do I have to do?"

Xavier nodded, a glint of approval in his eyes. "First, you finish your training here. Then, you follow my lead. But remember, Jack—once you step into this world, there's no going back. You'll be walking a fine line, balancing a normal life with a dangerous one. And if you slip, it's not just you who pays the price."

Jack frowned, his curiosity piqued. "And how exactly did you get into this line of work?"

Xavier's gaze drifted toward the open water, his expression momentarily softening. "It started a lot like this, actually. Scuba training was my gateway into the CIA. It was my favorite part of their training program—the freedom, the challenge, the quiet focus it demanded. When my time in active service started winding down, I decided to make diving my main occupation. It keeps me sharp, gives me peace... and, occasionally, it helps me find someone like you."

Jack swallowed hard, the weight of the decision pressing on him, his mind still doubting this was really happening. There were many risks involved, that is true. He could just say no, go back to his life and forget all of this had happened. But in his gut, he already knew he was in.

"Let's do it," he said.

Xavier clapped him on the shoulder. "Welcome to the shadows, Jack."

***

Things weren't as smooth as their boat sail that day when Jack started training to acquire the skills necessary to join the CIA. Though he had seen glimpses of his controlling nature during his scrubs diving lessons, Xavier Graves was a very strict tutor, his methods - designed to push him to his limits both physically and mentally. Learning how to be an undercover operative was about way more than developing skills—it was about transforming the way Jack thought, how he approached problems, and how he handled high-pressure situations - both on missions and in his day-to-day life.

Xavier's methods were precise, methodical, and almost clinical in their execution - every step had a purpose, every action a contingency. He was always following the rules by-the-book, and believed that preparation and discipline were the foundations of survival, part of the reason why he survived so long and kept going years later. "A good plan and a clear mind keep you alive," he'd often say. "Impulsivity and emotion get you killed." He would drill Jack relentlessly on procedure, from breaking down a room's layout in seconds to memorizing escape routes in hostile environments. Xavier's insistence on perfection sometimes grated on Jack, who wasn't naturally inclined toward such rigid structures.

Jack, by contrast, was a go-getter and a little more impulsive than Xavier wished for. He thrived on instinct and quick decision-making, always eager to take action rather than spend hours planning. He found Xavier's meticulous approach stifling at times, especially when it came to rehearsing scenarios down to the smallest detail. Jack had a simple and valid reasoning: the world didn't wait for you to perfect your plan; it required swift, decisive action.

This difference between their personalities often led to clashes during training sessions.

"Why do we need to go over this again?" Jack groaned one afternoon after they'd spent hours running through a mock infiltration scenario. "I already know the layout. Let's just do it."

Xavier raised an eyebrow, his calm demeanor unshaken. "Knowing the layout isn't enough. What if the intel's wrong? What if they've moved the target? What if you miss something because you're rushing in blind?"

Jack threw his hands up. "Then I'll adapt. That's what I do."

Xavier shot back, his voice sharp but controlled. "Fair enough. But keep in mind that you don't adapt under fire, Jack. You prepare before you're in the fire. That's how you stay alive."

Despite their differences, Jack couldn't deny that Xavier's methods worked. Over time, he learned to balance his natural instincts with the discipline Xavier drilled into him. He became a sharper, more efficient operative, capable of improvising when necessary, but always with a plan in mind. Still, Jack's tendency to follow his gut often put him at odds with Xavier, who remained frustrated by Jack's occasional recklessness.

"You're a loose cannon," Xavier said after one particularly heated argument during a field exercise. "You might get the job done, but you leave too many variables uncontrolled. One day, that's going to come back and bite you."

Jack smirked, brushing dirt off his hands. "Maybe. But at least the job gets done."

Over the years of working together, their differences became less of a source of conflict and they learned how to turn this into a positive way to complement their working relationship. It was a long process that took place on odd days when both Jack and Xavier were available and wouldn't raise suspicion. He learned how to be stealthy, how to shoot a gun, how to fight. Meanwhile, he also enrolled for training to become a firefighter - he got a degree in fire science, passed his physical test (which his CIA training helped a ton with) and became an EMT. His excuse to go training with Xavier was often under the pretext that he had "firefighter stuff to do" and Jen would happily buy this lie every time.

The turning point came months later. Xavier approached Jack with what he called "a favor"—a simple mission in Baja, California. "You will be in and out," Xavier had promised. "Nothing you can't handle."

Jack agreed, eager to prove himself and experience some action on the field. But the mission turned out to be anything but a simple task. What was supposed to be a quiet observation turned into a bloodbath when their team walked straight into an ambush. The cartel had been tipped off, and gunfire erupted in the night. Jack was in a position where he watched helplessly as several team members fell, their shouts drowned out by the chaos. This is where he met Mateo Vargas for the first time - he still remembers his burgundy shirt and neck chain, the way he spat while shouting commands to his loyal dogs of thugs in Spanish, and the way he brutally murdered innocent people. The screams of Jack's colleagues left a deep scar on his conscience, and a burning desire to avenge them. He almost got shot, too, when Xavier showed up and managed to get him out, dragging him through the darkness to safety. For Jack, safety was a distant memory now. The massacre that he witnessed was going to haunt him for years. Nightmares plagued his sleep, and every loud noise set his nerves on edge. It was his first real encounter with death, and it left a mark that even Xavier couldn't erase.

"You'll live," Xavier had said afterward, his tone gruff but not unkind. "And you'll learn. This won't break you, Jack. It'll make you stronger."

And it did—eventually. Jack channeled his pain into his work, both as a firefighter and as an undercover agent. But the shadows of that night never fully left him. The fire kept on burning, yet his actions became colder and more brutal. The more he saw the injustice in the world, the stronger he felt about serving that justice, even if it costs someone's life. Over the years, he also grew an obsession with using fire as a weapon. It was a cruel yet brilliant way to dispose of both people and evidence. His secret life and his personal pain cost sucked any sign of compassion out of his system, and he started experiencing a high from the fires. Playing God also meant he struggled to stay the same innocent, friendly man he once was. To avoid questions he didn't want to give an answer to, he distanced himself - from everyone he knew. Sometimes he struggled to sleep at night, the flames and remorse haunting his thoughts, which were forever busy with the question: "What is right and wrong?"

Back in Berkeley, Jack resumed his life as a firefighter, throwing himself into the structure and camaraderie of the station. It grounded him, gave him purpose. But by night, or on his days off work, he continued his covert missions, becoming more skilled, more ruthless, with every operation. The hardest part was keeping it all from Jen. She was his anchor, his safe haven, the person who believed in him more than anyone else ever had. But how could he tell her the truth? That while she thought he was out saving lives, he was also taking them in the shadows? He kept his secrets, convincing himself it was to protect her - and in fact it was, even if it's to keep her thoughts free of the burden he had to carry and the fear of the unpredictable future. Now, years later, he often wondered if that had been a mistake. Would Jen have tried to talk him out of it? Would she have seen the toll it was taking on him and stopped him before it was too late?

Now, she was gone, and the weight of those unanswered questions pressed heavily on Jack's shoulders.

***

The alarm clock hit 6am and BBC Radio 4 pierced through the quiet of Jack's bedroom. He lifted his hand and tried snoozing it without opening his eyes, turning on his side and hugging the pillow once more. *Five more minutes,* he thought. Then the pain hit him with the speed of light. He felt the swelling on his face, back, and arms. He ran his fingers through his brow, feeling a patch of blood that has now hardened and felt harsh against his skin, like rough sandpaper. His desire to steal five more minutes of peaceful sleep might not be the best of ideas right now. "I'll need a shower and a lot of painkillers to get through today," he said to himself with a groan. Every step towards the bathroom was a struggle, his body aching and his ears ringing.

The shower hissed as the water came to life, and with it - the thoughts about Vargas's cunning face rushed to him as quickly as the drops ran down his skin. Jack leaned against the cool tiles, his forehead pressed against the wall, as steam clouded the bathroom mirror and blurred the edges of reality, while the warm water was washing away the grime and sweat of another mission. He wished it could blur the memories, too - the face of Vargas, the loss of his friend and trusted colleague, the regrets and the desire for a simpler life. He wanted to serve justice so badly, yet he admitted to himself that a big part of him craved peace.

Vargas wasn't just a criminal - he was a disease infecting everything he touched. His network spread like ivy, gripping the foundations of his city and choking out any chance for peace. Jack rinsed the soap from his body, but no amount of scrubbing could erase the bloodstains in his memory. As he stepped out of the shower and caught a glimpse of himself in the fogged-up mirror, he almost didn't recognize the man staring back at him. His eyes were hollow, his face bruised, and the faint scar above his brow—the one from that first mission in Baja, California—stood out like an old wound, refusing to heal. It was Vargas who took the lives of all of his teammates that night. He was a snake, and Jack had to sever the head. Suddenly, a thought occurred. The memory of the conversation he had with Matteo last night resurfaced from the bottom of his conscience and got clearer the more the steam cleared from that mirror. *What did they mean, that the car was unrecognizable? Was Jen's death not an accident? -* Jack stopped and stared in his own image, questioning if he dared to open that door again. He never truly got closure about Jen's death, and not knowing who to blame festers and destroys you, like cancer. He toweled off and wrapped the fabric around his waist, padding barefoot into the kitchen, where the early morning light bled through the blinds. Ellie was curled up on the sofa, still wearing last night's clothes, a throw blanket draped over her shoulders. She had fallen asleep waiting for him. The air was crisp and filled with the distant hum of the city waking up. He could hear the faint drone of a garbage truck and the occasional bark of a dog. To anyone else, it was another normal, sunny day in Berkeley. But for Jack, it was another day to stay one step ahead of his enemies.

The smell of brewing coffee filled the room, earthy and bitter, the kind of aroma that promised solace but never quite delivered. At the stove, Jack flipped a pancake with practiced ease, the sizzle of batter mingling with the hum of the morning. His black coffee sat within reach on the counter, its warmth comforting as he took occasional sips between flipping pancakes and stirring scrambled eggs. For now, the simple routine of breakfast grounded him—a moment of normalcy before the chaos inevitably returned. He glanced at Ellie, almost with a hint of jealousy of how unaware she was of the chaos circling her father's life. *She is so innocent,* Jack thought, though he knew it wouldn't last for long. Not with Vargas still out there, especially not now that he has seen Jack's face. Her life could be in danger, and Jack would do anything to protect her. He could hear her slowly waking up and yawning. He sighed, glancing over his shoulder as he plated the pancakes. He knew that a hard conversation was coming.

Ellie stirred, rubbing her eyes groggily before looking toward the kitchen. Her voice was quiet, still heavy with sleep. "Hey, Dad, where were you? I was worried," she murmured. "I tried waiting up for you last night..."

Jack set a plate on the table. "Sorry, kiddo. I came in really late. I didn't want to wake you," he admitted, his voice low, in a desperate attempt to mask the severity of last night's actions.

Ellie hesitated for a moment before pulling the blanket tighter around her shoulders. She stood up and walked into the kitchen, her bare feet padding softly against the tile. Then, she saw his face and her expression changed instantly. "Dad... what...what happened to you?"

Jack knew what she was looking at. The faint bruising along his jaw, the cut near his temple, the exhaustion carved into his features. He looked away, focusing on pouring syrup over the pancakes like it was the most important task in the world. "It's *nothing*," he said, but as he spoke, he felt a pang of guilt for lying so blatantly.

She stepped closer, crossing her arms. "Doesn't look like 'nothing' to me. What happened? Are you okay?"

Jack sighed, running a hand over his face. He didn't have the energy for this—not after the night he'd had, not with Vargas still a threat. "Yes, I'm fine... In a couple of days, I will be as good as new. Now eat your breakfast, it's getting cold…" As he spoke, Jack couldn't help but notice how much Ellie's furrowed brow reminded him of her mother—how she too would question him with that same insightful gaze that seemed to cut right through him.

"No," she shot back, crossing her arms in a sign of protest. Her defiance made something tighten in Jack's chest. She was getting older, sharper. She saw through his excuses too easily now. "Not until you tell me what's going on."

Her insistence was a trait he admired, yet feared. It meant she wouldn't back down, not now, not ever. Jack let out a slow breath. He let out a slow breath. "I had a long night, that's all."

Ellie scoffed. "Yeah, no kidding. You look like you went ten rounds with a grizzly bear."

Jack almost smiled at that, but it faded quickly as he turned away, picking up his coffee and taking a sip. As he did, he wondered if keeping her in the dark was really protecting her or just isolating her further. "You don't have to worry about me, kid. It was an accident at work, nothing more," He said, offering a small, reassuring smile. But his gaze flicked away for a second, betraying the memory that lingered just beneath the surface. "We responded to a fire at an old warehouse. Standard procedure—or at least, it should have been." He ran a thumb along the rim of his cup, staring into the dark liquid as if it held the answer. "But there were still people inside. Not the kind who needed rescuing—the kind who didn't want us there. It got messy fast, but we handled it. Just a few bruises, nothing I can't shake off, okay?" He took a breath, steadying himself. "I'm fine, really. Just part of the job sometimes." But as he said it, the tension in his shoulders didn't quite ease.

Ellie exhaled sharply, frustrated. "You keep saying that, but I do worry. You disappear, you come back looking like this, and I'm supposed to just pretend it's fine?"

Jack leaned against the counter, rubbing the back of his neck. His body ached, his mind was still replaying last night's events, but here was Ellie—his daughter, the only piece of Jen he had left—staring at him with concern written all over her face. If he keeps being distant, he might lose her. "Ellie," he said carefully, his tone almost apologetic, "I know it's hard. But some things... you don't need to know. At least not for now. "

Her jaw clenched. "That's not fair."

Jack sighed, setting his coffee down. He wanted to keep her safe. He wanted to shield her from the world he lived in, from the weight he carried. But Ellie wasn't a little girl anymore. She was asking questions he wasn't sure he had answers for. "You just have to trust me," he said finally.

Ellie's eyes searched his face for a long moment before she nodded stiffly. "Fine," she muttered, grabbing a fork and stabbing at her pancakes with a clear sense of annoyance.

Jack sighed, rubbing his temples in a desperate desire to stop feeling like he was failing his daughter. The day was already off to a rough start. And the ghosts of last night weren't done haunting him yet. His phone buzzed on the counter, pulling him out of his thoughts. The screen lit up with a familiar name: *Xavier Graves, Scuba Instructor*. He hesitated for a moment before picking up the phone. *I wonder what he's on to now.*

"Morning, Jack," Xavier said, his voice as calm and calculated as ever. "We need to meet. Now."

Jack walked briskly away from the living room and towards the backyard so that Ellie couldn't hear his conversation. He whispered carefully, "Not a good time to talk, Xave. Is this about last night?"

Xavier didn't answer right away, and Jack could picture him leaning back in his chair, thinking through every word before speaking, his silence easily misinterpreted as judgment. "It's bigger than that. Vargas knows you're after him, and you've drawn attention to yourself. But there is more to it. You'd like to hear what I have to say. In person. Meet me at the usual spot in 30 minutes."

The line went dead.

Jack exhaled and lowered the phone, staring at the glowing screen until it dimmed and the reflection of his own tired eyes stared back at him.

Back in the kitchen, before he could fully process the call, Ellie's voice broke the silence. "Who was that?"

Jack didn't answer and drained the last of his coffee, then kissed Ellie on the forehead before heading to his room to change. "Gotta go, kiddo."

"Where are you going? Work doesn't start for another hour?"

"There is something I need to take care of first."

"Does it have anything to do with the mayor?"

Jack's head snapped up. Ellie stood by the kitchen island, her fork hovering over her plate, eyes sharp and narrowed. "What?" he asked cautiously.

Ellie bit her lip. "I saw the protest on TV last night. I know you were out. Was it because of that? Does it have anything to do with the mayor?"

For a split second, Jack froze. *How much did she know?* Was she connecting the dots? "Ellie, you shouldn't be worrying about things like this, and you should definitely not watch this kind of stuff at night," he said carefully.

"So that's a yes," she replied, crossing her arms. "I'm not stupid, Dad."

Jack sighed and raked his fingers through his hair, searching for the right words. "I didn't say that. It's just...um...complicated."

"It's always complicated with you," Ellie muttered, stabbing her pancake again. "But you won't tell me anything. I am not a child, you know."

Jack looked at her for a moment, the weight of the situation pressing down on him. But how could he tell her the truth without putting her in danger? His phone buzzed again, a sharp reminder of the conversation he couldn't avoid. "I need to go, but we'll talk later, okay?" he said, grabbing his phone and slipping it into his jacket.

Ellie's eyes flickered with frustration, but she didn't press him further. She stormed back into her room, her safe space, and shut the door. Jack hesitated. He wanted to stay and work this out; he wanted to say something else, something that would ease the tension from their earlier conversation—but what could he say? Nothing he said would fix this, at least not right now. He slipped on a pair of worn jeans, a black T-shirt, and his leather jacket—the one Jen used to tease him about, saying it made him look like an action movie star. He smiled, wondering what she will have to say about this now.

He turned to grab his keys when something on the counter caught his eye—a letter. He picked it up, flipping it over. His breath hitched when he saw the sender—Ellie's school. Jack frowned, setting down his keys as he tore open the envelope. His eyes scanned the letter quickly, his grip tightening with every word.

Dear Mr. Singer,

We are reaching out regarding your daughter's recent attendance record and behavioral concerns observed over the past few weeks. Ellie has been fre-

quently absent or leaving school early, without proper authorization. Additionally, we have noted signs of disruptive behavior in class and a reluctance to engage in her coursework.

We understand that adolescence can bring challenges, but we strongly encourage a discussion regarding these concerns. Please contact the administration at your earliest convenience to arrange a meeting.

Sincerely,

Dean Margaret Collins Berkeley High School

Jack let the words sink in, setting the letter down on the counter. *Attendance issues? Leaving school early?* That wasn't like Ellie. Sure, she could be stubborn, but skipping class? Acting out? Something wasn't right. And after the week he'd had, he wasn't sure he had the patience to dance around the truth, but at the same time didn't know whether to approach this calmly or let the guilt and anger simmer over. He knocked on Ellie's bedroom door with hesitation. "Ellie," Jack said, voice low but firm.

She stopped, looking up at him. "What?" He held up the letter. "We need to talk."

Ellie's expression shifted immediately, walls going up as she crossed her arms. "About what?"

Jack didn't let her play dumb. He slapped the letter onto the table; the sound cutting through the silence like a whip. "Your school reached out about your attendance. You wanna tell me what's going on, Ellie?"

She blinked, her lips parting slightly before she pressed them into a tight line. "Nothing. I'm fine." As she spoke, her fingers unconsciously played with the ear of a well-worn stuffed rabbit—a relic from her younger years that she hadn't quite been able to part with.

Jack's patience snapped. "Fine? Skipping class, causing trouble? Why didn't you come to me if you were struggling? I would've helped you. Been there for you"

Ellie's jaw tightened. "Help me? Well, that would be pretty damn hard, considering you're never here. And from what I can see, you can barely help yourself, dad."

"Ellie... language." His voice softened, but the tension in it was undeniable.

She glared at him, her eyes blazing with frustration. The tension between them was thick, suffocating. "I didn't tell you because you don't tell me anything, either. You disappear for *days*, come back looking like you got hit by a truck, and I'm supposed to sit here and act like everything's fine?"

Jack froze, her words hitting him harder than any punch Vargas had thrown. "I worry about you, Dad," Ellie said, her voice cracking. "You're all I have left, and you won't even let me in. How is that fair?"

Jack's shoulders sagged as the fight drained out of him. He ran a hand over his face, guilt settling deep in his chest. He had been so focused on protecting her that he hadn't realized how much he was shutting her out. "Ellie..." he started, but she shook her head.

"You don't trust me," she whispered.

Jack stepped closer, but she backed away. The distance between them felt heavier than ever.

"It's not about trust," Jack said softly. "I know you're worried, and you have every right to be. But it's complicated—things at work, they aren't always what they seem. I'm just trying to keep you safe."

Ellie's eyes filled with tears, but she quickly wiped them away. "Maybe I don't want to be safe. Maybe I just want my dad back."

Jack felt the weight of her words crush him. He opened his mouth to say something, anything, but no words came. His throat tightened, his thoughts scrambled—every excuse, every half-truth, seemed suddenly inadequate.

Ellie grabbed her backpack and headed for the door. "Ellie, wait—"

She stopped, hand on the doorknob. "I have to get ready for school. I'm going to be late."

The door closed behind her before he could respond. Jack stood in the empty corridor, his heart pounding. He had faced fires, criminals, and cartels, but nothing terrified him more than the thought of losing Ellie. Her words echoed in his mind, a painful reminder of how much damage he'd already done by shutting her out. He had to find a way to fix this. Before it was too late. Taking a deep breath, he grabbed his jacket and keys from the counter, folding the letter back into his pocket. He hesitated for just a second, casting one last glance at the house—the place where he should have felt grounded, but lately, only felt like he was slipping further away.

With that, he stepped out into the brisk morning air, which hit him like a slap. Somehow, the city felt different today - a cooler breeze and a heavy ocean scent filled up the air, as if it knew what Jack was going through.

The city was just waking up, the hum of traffic growing in the distance, the faint smell of street vendors preparing breakfast wafting through the breeze. But Jack barely noticed any of it. His mind churned, filled with questions he couldn't answer and problems he couldn't solve.

The drive to the meet-up point was silent, the only sound coming from the hum of the engine and the occasional driver having a mild road rage. "God, if you only knew there were much bigger problems in the world than someone cutting you off," - Jack said to himself with frustration. His mind kept replaying Vargas's words: *Last I heard, your car was unrecognizable that day.* He needed answers, and he needed them fast. Because while he had dedicated his life to fighting fire, both literal and metaphorical. He had made a career of fighting fires, but now the flames were closing in from all sides. He *had* to figure this out before everything burned to the ground. As he pulled into the usual parking space outside East Bay Diving Academy, the fog clung to the waterfront like a veil, waiting to be lifted and show the secrets that lie underneath it, deep and dark as the ocean. Xavier was waiting by a stack of crates, looking sharp and serious, his hands in his pockets and his expression unreadable.

Jack stepped out of the car and approached him, the sound of his boots muffled by the damp ground. "What's so urgent? It better be good. I just turned down my daughter again, who, by the way, is starting to dislike me for my constant disappearances."

Xavier nodded toward the crates, where a manila folder rested like a time bomb waiting to go off. "She'll be fine. You knew what you signed up for. How about you tell me everything that went down at the docks before I came? You weren't yourself last night. I didn't have the heart to ask you questions."

Jack sighed. "Mateo Vargas was there for a reason. It wasn't just a routine shipment. He wouldn't bother showing his face if it were. I am pretty sure he wanted to send a message."

"To you?"

"To Maverick..." Xavier's voice was steady, but there was an edge of tension beneath it.

Jack nodded. "Yeah. He wasn't there for the shipment itself. He wanted to see who had the guts to get in his way. I am pretty certain of it. He had more men than ever, and a pretty solid escape plan - I mean, the guy practically vanished into thin air."

Xavier cursed under his breath. "That's what I was afraid of. You were too exposed, Jack. And that Mexican cop? Why did you have to go and be a hero? She could've seen your face...

"She didn't"—Jack says.

"She was working alongside the DEA in a joint operation. The local police, Mexican federal agents, and the DEA all swarming that place. Why the hell were Mexican cops even at the warehouse in the first place? The last thing we need is them connecting you to the fires."

Jack looked out the window, fingers drumming against his knee. "So what now?"

Xavier rubbed the back of his neck, his movements unusually tense and restless. "I've got intel you're not going to like. He nodded toward the crates, where a manila folder rested like a time bomb waiting to go off. Jack picked it up, flipping it open to reveal photos of Mayor Quinn shaking hands with Mateo Vargas outside a private estate. His blood ran cold.

"They're not just working together," Xavier said. "They're partners. The fires, the protests, the drug shipments through Oakland Harbor—it's all connected. And you, my friend, as usual, are right in the middle of it."

Jack clenched his jaw, his mind spinning with possibilities, his face a wide palette of emotions. "I knew it. Why didn't you bring this to me sooner?"

"Because this isn't just about you anymore, Jack. Vargas' reach might extend further than the Mayor. We both know he's tied to the cartel, but we don't have enough to bring him down. And he's getting bolder. Someone higher up might be involved, and covering for him. This is why it took so long to get to the bottom of this. Look, Jack, I think you might have to step aside for a while. They're watching your house."

Jack's breath hitched, and for a moment, the world tilted. "What did you just say?"

"You heard me well," Xavier replied, his steady gaze studying Jack's reaction. "You've pissed off the wrong people, and now they're looking for leverage. Ellie is the perfect leverage."

The words hung between them like a storm cloud ready to burst. Jack's mind raced, thinking of every possible way to protect her, to eliminate the threat before it got too close. He had fought fires, taken lives, and buried secrets, but nothing had ever terrified him more than the thought of losing Ellie. "We need to end this," Jack said, his voice low and dangerous. "Now."

"If we do, we are going to do it my way this time. No improvisations, no risky missions, and certainly no rushing into things," - Xavier said calmly, yet with an unusual shift in his demeanor - he seemed more intense, leaning forward as he spoke.

"Wait, how did they even know how to find me? The pieces are not connected together. What is it that you are not telling me, Xavier?"

"Someone within our network must have tipped them off."

"What, we have a snitch now?" -Jack's blood started to boil, his lack of control over the situation taking over his rational thoughts.

"Look, all I know for now, Jack, is you're better off keeping your head down. Let me handle this. And don't do anything stupid. Wait for my call."

Jack walked back to his car, slammed the door and sat in there for a brief moment, his thoughts occupied with calculations and fear. The engine purred as he drove off towards Fire Station #5, where he had a 48-hour shift to pull. The sun shone through the clouds lingering overhead, his hands gripping the wheel tighter than they needed to, his knuckles whitening with tension. The conversation with Xavier replayed in his head like a broken record, but he couldn't afford to let his mind drift too far. Not now. Not with Ellie. Jack stared at her number on the dashboard screen, his finger hovering over the call button. Their last conversation echoed in his mind—her accusing words, "Maybe I just want my dad back." He sighed, pushing the thought aside. He couldn't afford another fight. Not today. He tapped the button, hoping for a better conversation this time. It rang twice before her voice came through, soft and slightly groggy.

"Hey, Dad," Ellie said softly, stifling a yawn. "Heyyy, kiddo. You sleep okay?"

"Yeah, I guess." Her tone had that teenage mix of half-truths; she was trying to act tougher than she felt, but Jack knew better. "Well, at least she got something from me," Jack thought.

"Listen, honey," he said, glancing at the clock. "I know things have been... tense between us lately. But I really don't like the idea of you being alone all weekend. I'm headed to the station, but I can call your aunt Meg to come and pick you up. I thought you might want to stay at their place for a few days while I'm at work. What do you think?"

Ellie paused briefly.

"Ellie?"

She then broke the silence, "Dad, I'm fourteen. I don't need a babysitter."

Jack chuckled softly. "I know, I know... But humor me, okay? I don't like you being alone all weekend. You've got plenty of time to be independent once you're older."

Ellie sighed, but it wasn't the kind of sigh that led to an argument. "Fine. But you owe me."

"How about we spend a day in the park when I am off work? We'll grab some ice cream, feed the ducks, maybe even get the bikes out. Like we used to?"

"That's bribery, dad, but okay, it sounds good." she said, her voice lighter now. "Be safe at work."

"I will." Jack hesitated before speaking again, the image of Xavier's warning flashing in his mind. "And, Ellie?"

"Yeah?"

"Also, um, make sure the doors are locked... Don't let anyone in unless it's your aunt Meg, alright? She should be there soon..."

There was a pause, brief but noticeable. "Okay, Dad."

"Good. I'll see you tonight. I love you." He ended the call and let out a long breath, as if hanging up allowed him to exhale the fears he didn't dare voice aloud. He needed to stay focused on Vargas and the mayor. "But you also need to be a good father, Jack," he imagined Jen's gentle voice saying to him as a reminder.

***

Ellie placed her phone on the nightstand and flopped back onto her bed, staring up at the ceiling as her father's words echoed in her mind. *Lock the doors. Don't let anyone in.* He always sounded so worried these days, even when he tried to hide it. She didn't remember him being like this before Mom died.

She sighed, brushing a strand of hair out of her face, and forced herself to sit up. The morning sunlight filtered through the curtains, casting soft golden streaks across her room. She pulled them to allow the sun to illuminate her room, the warm light bathing everything in a tranquil glow that offered peace and protection. She reached for her journal, the one with the worn leather cover that Mom had given her on her last birthday. Ellie traced her fingers over the handwritten message at the start—Explore the beauty of your mind, Love, Mom—and opened it to the next blank page.

Her pen hovered for a moment before she began to write:

I miss the way things used to be. When Dad would laugh more, when Mom was here to keep everything from falling apart. Sometimes it feels like I'm the only one who notices how broken everything is. Dad thinks he's handling it, but I see it. The way he stares off into space when he thinks I'm not looking. The way he tries too hard to make me happy, as if cooking lasagna can fix everything.

She paused, tapping the pen against the page.

I don't blame him. I know he's trying. But I wish he'd talk to me instead of acting like he has to protect me from the world. I'm not a little kid anymore. I love him, but sometimes I feel like we are total strangers, like he is having a second life that I know nothing about.

The words came faster now, her thoughts spilling onto the page like they'd been waiting for this exact moment.

Sometimes I feel guilty for missing Mom so much, like it's a betrayal to Dad. But how can I not miss her? She was the one who understood, even when I didn't feel like talking. She would just sit with me and let me be. And now...

Ellie stopped, wiping a tear off her cheek before it could fall onto the paper. She closed the journal and set it aside, rubbing her eyes as she stood up.

An hour later, the doorbell rang, pulling Ellie away from the moment and back to reality. She pulled on a pair of jeans and a hoodie, gazing at herself in the mirror. Her reflection stared back - her eyes glistening like pearls, reflecting her sadness and loneliness that never seemed to go away. She didn't want to admit it, but she loved having aunt Meghan around. It made her feel less empty, even if she'd never say that to Dad. She wanted to be strong for both of them, to show him she is deserving of being called a "grown-up". The doorbell rang again, and Ellie ran down the hallway and peeked through the window to see aunt Meghan's familiar smiling face.

"Morning, Ellie," aunt Meg said, stepping inside. "Hope you are ready for a weekend of board games and bad TV."

Ellie chuckled, slowly shutting the door behind them. "As long as you don't try and win."

"Are you all packed, or do you need a hand?"

"Almost ready!" Ellie said, her desire to stay independent showing up once more. For the first time that morning, Ellie felt a little less alone. As she packed her essentials in her backpack, her mind drifted back to her dad, to the way his voice sounded on the phone - like he was worried and holding something back. She didn't know what it was, but one thing she knew for sure - whatever it was, it wasn't just about work. She was old enough to sense that.

Chapter 7

Sofía hadn't planned on staying in the U.S. for long, but plans had a way of unraveling when bullets were involved. After the chaos at the warehouse—the shootout, Vargas's men, and the searing pain from the bullets that struck her—she found herself confined to a hospital bed. The bulletproof vest had done its job, but not without consequences. The shot to her chest had left her with a bruised rib, possibly fractured, and her shoulder throbbed from where a stray bullet had grazed her skin. Nothing life-threatening, but enough to warrant at least two days in the hospital for observation. Routine, they called it. As if waking up sore and breathless after dodging death was anything but. She spent the whole day in the sterile room, drifting in and out of sleep, with the rhythmic beeping of the heart monitor keeping her tethered to reality. Her mind, however, refused to rest. Even with the painkillers dulling the ache, her thoughts remained sharp, circling back to Vargas, the Sangre Cartel, and the loose ends she hadn't tied up.

She awoke with a start, her breath hitching as she sat up in bed. The remnants of the dream clung to her like a thick fog—a pair of hands pulling her to safety, the sting of Vargas's bullets hitting her chest despite the protective vest. The impact had knocked the air from her lungs, leaving her gasping, her shoulder burning where a stray bullet had grazed her.

And through the haze of pain, there had been a man's voice, steady and warm, telling her it was all going to be okay. But no matter how hard she tried to picture his face, it remained blurred, obscured by the smoke of her subconscious, as if her mind was keeping that moment just out of reach. She could still feel the rough grip of his hands, the scrape of gravel beneath her, and the pounding of her heart as he shielded her from danger. And yet, his face—Jack's face—refused to come into focus. She ran a hand through her hair and exhaled sharply. *Who was he?* The question had plagued her since that night.

She couldn't wait any longer. She pulled her jacket carefully over her sore shoulder and stepped outside the hospital, the midday sun warming her skin. She had lost time here, time she couldn't afford to waste. But now, she was back on her feet, and it was time to pick up the trail Vargas thought he had left behind. With a determined breath, she tightened her grip on her bag and made her way toward the car, waiting to take her to the next lead.

***

Sofía stormed through the sliding glass doors of the DEA office, her boots echoing against the polished floor. A wave of colleagues glanced up from their desks, some offering sympathetic nods, others whispering to each other as she passed. She ignored them all. Near the entrance to the operations room, Agent Tom Warton stepped into her path, his hands raised as if to block her.

"You shouldn't be here," Tom said, his tone cautious. "You need rest, Sofía."

"I'll rest when we catch every last one of them," she snapped, brushing past him and into the main operations hub.

The room was a flurry of activity—agents on phones, analysts combing through surveillance footage, and stacks of files spread across desks. But Sofía had one target in mind: the man in interrogation room 2. She marched toward the observation window, where a one-way mirror allowed her to view the suspect inside. A low-level thug with ties to the Vargas cartel sat slouched in his chair, arms crossed, his face blank. The same smug expression he'd had for the past two hours. Sofía gritted her teeth and pushed open the door to the interrogation room.

The man looked up lazily, smirking as his eyes scanned her with mocking amusement. "Oh, a lady cop? They must be really desperate out there."

Sofía didn't flinch. She stepped inside, letting the door slam shut behind her. "Desperate enough to put you exactly where you belong," she shot back, her voice cool but sharp as a blade.

He chuckled and leaned back, the cuffs around his wrists clinking faintly against the metal chair. "You can play tough all you want, sweetheart, but I've seen worse than you."

She leaned over the table, her palms flat against the cold metal. "You think this is a joke? Vargas isn't going to save you, and if you think your court- appointed lawyer is going to get you out of this, think again."

The thug chuckled. "Lady, you've got nothing on me. I was just in the wrong place at the wrong time."

Sofía's eyes narrowed. "Wrong place, wrong time? You were in the middle of a shootout during an illegal weapons transfer. Witnesses saw you fleeing the warehouse."

"Fleeing?" He grinned, leaning back in his chair until the handcuffs tugged against his wrists. "I was running for my life. You can't prove I had anything to do with that place."

Sofía's patience snapped. She grabbed the chair opposite him and slammed it down as she sat; the legs scraping against the concrete floor. She leaned in, her eyes narrowing. "How long have you been working for Vargas? Months? Years? Long enough to know what happens to people who cross him?"

The thug shrugged, a smirk curling at the edge of his lips. "Long enough to know that you shouldn't waste any more time on me."

Frustration clawed at her, but she pushed it down. She wasn't going to give him the satisfaction of seeing her lose control. Instead, she stood abruptly, her chair scraping back across the floor as she glared down at him one last time. "You won't be so smug when Vargas cuts you loose to save his own skin." She turned and walked toward the door.

"Leaving already?" he taunted, his voice dripping with amusement, as if her departure was exactly what he wanted.

Sofía paused for just a second, her hand resting on the doorknob. "Enjoy the silence while it lasts. I'm just getting started." And with that, she walked out, letting the heavy door close behind her. She entered the observation room where Warton and two other agents were watching through the glass. The tension in her shoulders hadn't eased. If anything, it had grown worse.

"I told you," Warton said, arms folded. "He's never going to talk. Especially now with that lawyer coming down here."

Sofía rubbed her temples, trying to think. "What about putting a tail on him? If we can't get anything out of him in here, we'll track him on the outside."

"You know we can't do that. The lawyer will raise hell if he finds out we're tailing his client without cause. And right now, we don't have enough evidence to get a warrant."

"We can make it work," Sofía argued. "We know he's connected to Vargas. He'll slip up if we watch him long enough."

Before Warton could respond, his supervisor, Agent Abbott, entered the room. He wasn't smiling. "We're letting him go," Abbott said flatly.

Sofía's head snapped toward him. "What? You can't be serious."

"His lawyer's already making noise about unlawful detainment. We don't have enough to hold him, and the brass doesn't want this blowing back on us. Let him walk."

"You're just going to let him disappear back into the cartel's hands?" she asked, incredulous.

"We don't have a choice, Sofía," Abbott said firmly. "And I don't want to hear about you trying to tail him off the books either. Do you understand me?"

Sofía's jaw clenched. "Crystal clear."

Abbott nodded and left the room, leaving an unbearable silence in his wake.

Warton glanced at Sofía. "Don't do anything stupid." She didn't respond. Her mind was already made up.

Later, as Sofía stood at the second-floor window of the precinct, her gaze locked on the entrance below. The late afternoon sun cast long shadows across the pavement, but it did little to brighten her mood. She watched as the thug strolled out of the building, his cuffs removed, freedom granted—for now. A smug grin stretched across his face, as if he had already won. His lawyer followed closely behind, speaking to him in low tones, their conversation short but confident. Whatever deal they had struck in there was enough to give him the upper hand, at least temporarily. Sofía's fingers tightened around the edge of the blinds, her knuckles turning white as she tracked their movements. The lawyer gave the thug a pat on the shoulder and a parting word before heading toward a sleek black sedan parked along the curb. But it wasn't the lawyer that concerned her.

It was the car waiting for the thug. A beat-up, dark SUV idled at the edge of the lot, its windows tinted too dark to see inside. The driver, a man wearing sunglasses and a baseball cap pulled low, barely glanced up as the thug slid into the backseat. Something about the way the vehicle lingered a moment longer before pulling away made Sofía's instincts hum. She recognized the type—a vehicle used by people who preferred to stay under the radar.

As the SUV disappeared down the street, she released the blinds and grabbed her phone. If the DEA wouldn't tail him, she would find some-body who would. "Dispatch," she said, her voice steady but sharp, "I need a tail on the black SUV leaving the precinct now." Her gut told her this wasn't just a ride home—it was a link in the chain that could lead her straight to Vargas. Because if there was one thing Sofía Calderón couldn't stand, it was loose ends. And she was about to tie this one off—whether her boss approved or not. After placing the call to dispatch, Sofía gathered her things and headed back inside the precinct. Her mind was already calculating her next move, but her phone buzzed before she could get far. Marco.

"Calderón," she answered briskly, bracing for bad news.

"Sofía," her partner's voice crackled through the line, "I hate to do this to you, but we need you back in Mexico. Chief's orders. Something's come up. He said it's important."

Her stomach twisted. "What now?"

"He wants a full debrief on the warehouse shooting and your time here and there was something else, but he wouldn't tell me. He wasn't exactly flexible about it," Marco added. "He said you'd understand."

She could read between the lines—this wasn't just about a routine debrief. Her boss didn't summon her without reason, and if Marco was being this vague, it meant either they had new intel, or her investigation was stepping on the wrong toes. "Fine," she said, her voice firm. "I'll be on the next flight."

After ending the call, she packed quickly, her mind still circling the thug, the lawyer, and the dodgy SUV. Whatever her boss wanted, she'd deal with it—but this investigation wasn't over.

***

Detective Sofia Calderón leaned over her desk, staring at the map pinned to the wall. Red circles marked the locations of the arson sites, each one aligning almost perfectly with properties tied to the Sangre Cartel. Her eyes burned from hours of poring over files and reports, but she didn't care. Somewhere in this mess of evidence lay the truth—and she wasn't going to stop until she found it. The debrief had been mostly procedural, but something about the way her boss had rushed her back didn't sit right.

As she worked late into the night, a new realization started to form. The burned locations followed a pattern. Properties being emptied, families forced out, or individuals who posed a threat to cartel influence. The fires weren't accidents. They were cleanup jobs. And she was starting to see exactly how deep this went. Her eyes flicked to a printout on her desk—an article about American firefighters donating a staggering amount of equipment to Mexican stations. At first, it seemed harmless enough: a feel-good story about Americans helping their neighbors. But every time one of the visiting units delivered equipment, a fire broke out within days, sometimes hours. Coincidence? She didn't think so. Sofia picked up the phone and dialed a local fire chief in Los Cerros. "I need to know who accompanied Álvaro to the inspection on the villa in Ensenada last year..."

"Let me check the roster," the chief replied. After a moment, he came back on the line. "A few gringos were with him that day. They were from one of the California departments that donated equipment recently."

Her pulse quickened. "Get me a list of all the fire units that have been down here in the past year."

The chief faxed over a document listing every team that had participated in operations or provided donations over the past year. Sofia skimmed through it, her finger trailing down the names. She called each department one by one, asking about personnel who had joined the cross-border operations. Most conversations led nowhere- until she dialed Jack's unit. The phone rang twice before someone picked up.

"Berkeley Fire Department, this is Jack speaking."

Sofia froze for a second, her heart thudding in her chest. *What was it about this voice that made her hair stand on end?*

"Hello, this is Detective Sofía Calderón with the Los Cerros Police Department. I'm investigating the collaboration between California fire units and our local departments here in Mexico over the past few years, and I need to confirm your agency's involvement. Could you provide details on whether your team was active in the region and if any of your crew members conducted an inspection at a villa in Ensenada?"

There was a brief pause on the other end of the line before Jack replied, his voice careful. "Uh, yeah... we were there a while back. Just a standard equipment delivery and safety inspection. I can fax over the dates when we've been in Mexico, if that helps."

"Right, thank you," Sofía said, her voice steady, masking the tension building inside her.

Jack cleared his throat slightly. "Is there anything else I can help you with, Detective?"

"Uhm. Not for now, but I appreciate your help, Jack," she replied. A subtle pause hung in the air before she added, "I'm sure we'll be in touch again soon."

After hanging up, Sofía sat down at her desk, tapping her pen against the stack of folders that had consumed her life for the past few weeks. The fax machine whirred to life, spitting out a series of papers marked with dates and locations of Jack's station's visits to Mexico. She scanned through them quickly, her finger trailing down the page until she stopped cold.

The dates matched perfectly—not only with the Ensenada fire, but with two others in nearby towns. Her pulse quickened as she pulled open one of the folders from her case files, cross-referencing Jack's station visits with the arson investigation logs. The more she compared, the more it clicked. Each fire had ignited within days of Jack's team being in the area, and the locations weren't random. Her fingers hovered over her phone, the temptation to call Marco gnawing at her, but she hesitated. Not yet. She needed more. She needed something solid before she could accuse someone like Jack Singer of being part of the problem—or worse, part of Vargas's operation. Over the next few days, Sofia kept digging. She questioned local police, combed through protest reports, and tracked connections between the cartel and city officials. Every lead brought her closer to the same names—the mayor, key Sangre Cartel leaders, and the firefighters who seemed to appear right before chaos struck. As she pieced it together, a troubling thought formed: What if the fires weren't just arson, but something bigger? What if they were a cover for something else entirely?

Her late brother had visited that house before the fire.... And now, Sofia wondered if the firefighter visits weren't about charity at all, but about cleaning up loose ends.

One night, while pouring over the case files, she had connected with a confidential informant who had worked with intelligence agencies in the past. "There's a rogue CIA agent operating under the radar," the informant warned. "I've heard whispers that he's involved in missions outside - official channels—missions where collateral damage isn't a concern." Sofia's fingers trembled as she ended the call. Could Jack be that agent? If he was, what did that make him—an undercover hero taking down the cartel or a villain who didn't care who got hurt in the process? Her brother's face flashed in her mind, and with it, the desire for justice. The deeper she dug, the more questions she uncovered—and the more resistance she faced.

One day, her boss called her into his office, his expression unreadable as he gestured for her to sit. Sofía reluctantly complied, folding her arms as she waited for the inevitable reprimand. "Sofia," he said, his tone heavy with warning. "We're not chasing this. You're looking for patterns that aren't there."

She tensed, her frustration barely contained. "They're there," she shot back. "These fires aren't random. And the cartel—"

He held up a hand to stop her, leaning forward slightly. "This isn't up for debate. We don't have the resources to take on that mayor or anyone connected to him. Focus on what we can prove."

But Sofia couldn't let it go. She opened her mouth to argue, but he cut her off. "I know you're dedicated, and that's exactly why I'm offering you something else. We've been thinking about this for a while. There's an open position in the Organized Crime Unit. It's a step up, more resources, more flexibility. But if you keep pulling at these threads without proof, you'll risk everything. Take the promotion. Let this case go."

The words hit her like a blow. A promotion should have felt like recognition, but right now, it felt like a bribe. A way to get her to drop the one case she couldn't let go. Her throat tightened, but she kept her composure. "So, what? I move to another unit and pretend these fires never happened?"

"You won't have to pretend," he said firmly. "Because without hard evidence, this case will disappear on its own."

Sofía stared at him for a long moment, weighing her options. If she said no, she'd be labeled a liability. If she said yes, she'd gain access to resources that could potentially help her finish what she started—but it would come at a cost. Finally, she stood, her expression cool and unreadable. "I'll think about it."

Her boss nodded, satisfied. But as she walked out of his office, Sofía already knew her decision. The fires weren't random, and Vargas was at the center of it. Promotion or not, she was going to see this investigation through— whether the department approved or not.

By the time she got home, the weight of the day hung heavy on her shoulders. She dropped her keys on the counter and slipped off her shoes, the cool tile floor soothing her tired feet. In the kitchen, she poured herself a generous glass of red wine, savoring the first sip before carrying it into the living room. Rocco perked up as she sat on the sofa. He wagged his tail lazily, resting his head on her lap as if sensing she needed the comfort. Sofía absentmindedly scratched behind his ears while flicking through channels on the TV. The soft hum of background noise was supposed to relax her, but her mind refused to quiet. After a few minutes of aimless scrolling, she exhaled sharply and set down her wineglass. "Enough of this," she muttered, gently shifting Rocco off her lap. The dog let out a soft whine before curling up in a ball on the floor. She grabbed her laptop from the coffee table and opened it, her fingers hesitating briefly over the keyboard before typing: Berkeley news. She wasn't even sure what she was looking for—maybe something about the mayor, or a clue linking Jack's visits to something bigger. But as she scrolled, one headline jumped out at her: *MAYOR'S GALA RETURNS NEXT WEEKEND TO HONOR CALIFORNIA FIREFIGHTERS FOR INTERNATIONAL COLLABORATIONS.*

Her eyes narrowed as she clicked on the article. The gala was a high-profile event, with politicians, community leaders, and even key figures from international organizations set to attend. And with the event specifically honoring California's firefighters, there was a strong chance Jack would be there—or at the very least, someone who could tell her more about him. She grabbed her phone and dialed a number from memory.

A friend picked up after a few rings, her voice warm and familiar. "Hey, Sofía! It's been so long. How is everything?"

"I know this is last minute, but could you watch Rocco for a couple of days next weekend? I've been dying for a spa getaway, and I finally have a chance to go."

"A spa weekend, huh?" her friend teased. "About time you took a break. Of course, I'll take him. He and Luna will have a blast together."

Sofía smiled, relieved. "Thanks. I owe you one."

After hanging up, she leaned back on the sofa, her mind already planning the next steps. She wasn't going to Berkeley to relax — she was going to find Jack Singer, connect the dots, and get the answers no one else seemed willing to look for. Rocco let out a small sigh from his spot on the floor, and Sofía reached down to pat his head. "Don't miss me too much," she said softly.

***

The smell of fresh coffee and burning toast filled the firehouse kitchen as the morning hum of activity picked up. Jack entered through the back door, the weight of his conversation with Xavier still pressing down on his shoulders. As B Shift was busy briefing C Shift and packing their bags, the firehouse was filled with the usual banter echoing off the walls. You could hear Abe's booming laugh, teasing Jay mercilessly about something or other, and Ria telling them both to grow up. "Home, sweet home," Jack thought, his worries now shifting from his morning encounter to the creation of a clever lie to explain his bruises. He dropped his bag by the lockers and grabbed a cup of coffee before making his way to the common room, where most of the crew was already gathered around the kitchen table. Abe was, as usual, the center of the conversation, leaning back in his chair with confidence.

"Jay, next time you're on the roof team, could you try not to make it look like Cirque du Soleil up there?"

"Abe, look man, at least I wasn't the one who almost lost their helmet during the drill."

"Hey, that's because I was moving fast. You, on the other hand, were still figuring out how your legs work."

Jack overheard their conversation from across the room and decided to stand up to the young fellow. "Cut him some slack, Abe. You were just as bad when you started."

"Yeah, but at least I had the decency to make it look cool."

Jack smiled faintly and took a seat at the far end of the table, nursing his coffee in silence as he observed the crew. It didn't take long for Abe to notice him.

"Well, look who finally decided to grace us with his presence - the Captain of the ship," Abe said, grinning. "What happened, Jack? Long night of beauty sleep, or did you lose a fight with a punching bag?"

Jack smirked. "You should see the other guy."

The crew chuckled, but Jack could feel Abe's gaze lingering on him longer than necessary, like a wild cat tracking a prey.

"Seriously, what happened? Did you end up in a bar fight?" Ria showed genuine concern, her innocent-looking face now one of worry and bemusement.

Jay chimed in, trying to defuse the tension in his innate desire for peace and his admiration to Jack. "C'mon, give the man a break. We all know Jack's tougher than he looks. Besides, we should be talking about how you saved the day at the docks, Abe."

Jack froze for half a second, his grip on the mug tightening, before he quickly realized he should mask his reaction. He was briefed about the fire at the docks, and acted as if he hadn't heard of it. Little did anyone know that he was the one who caused it, again. He took another sip of coffee, keeping his face neutral. "Oh, yeah, I heard the fire was so bad they called us for backup. What the hell was Abe doing at the docks? Last I checked, you weren't supposed to be on shift that night - or am I missing something?"

"That's right," exclaimed Ria, while standing up to clean her plate. "Everyone's been talking about it. Some big emergency, right? What exactly happened?", she turned around and fixed her gaze on Abe, the way a mother would look at her child and await explanation for its late arrival home.

Abe shrugged, leaning back in his chair and tilting his head to the right like it was no big deal. "Just doing my job, really. We got called in to help contain the fire before it spread to the warehouse district. Nothing fancy. Apparently some big action between the cartel and the police, but by the time we got there, everyone had vanished. I hear two of those cartel monkeys are put behind bars for questioning. The fire - clearly intentional and sloppy, nothing we haven't handled before. Though I did save Bob's ass from a falling beam - don't know what he was thinking, perhaps daydreaming about his wife's casserole again or something. Ah, you guys know how B Shift can be he-he." - he shrugged his shoulders again, in a humble manner that one who doesn't like to boast would do. Abe didn't like being too serious, though, and he knew which jokes clicked with his crew. "But hey, if you all want to build me a statue, I'm not going to stop you. There is enough space down there."

The group laughed again, but Jack's mind was elsewhere. On the outside, he tried to stay still because he knew pretty darn well that fake smiles didn't work for him, meanwhile underneath his freckled skin the fire was burning again, spreading to every cell and every limb of his body, which now felt paralyzed. He replayed the night at the docks, going over every detail, every step. He was sure he hadn't left anything behind—but Abe was acting strange, and it wasn't like him to be this... cold. His intuition was telling him he knew something, but what could he possibly know? Is he being paranoid?

Abe's eyes flicked to Jack, and for a moment, there was a charged silence between them. Then, with that same easygoing tone, Abe said, "Hey, Jack. What were you up to that night, anyway? Sleeping tight or starting bar fights?"

While the crew took this as another one of Abe's jokes, Jack sensed a tone of suspiciousness; he knew Abe well enough to read between the lines. He chuckled nervously, leaning back in his chair and crossing his hands together, mirroring Abe's posture. "Best sleep I've had in weeks."

"Oh, yeah?" Abe smiled, but it didn't reach his eyes. "I bet you did, old man."

The conversation was interrupted by the radio dispatch, which gave Jack an opportunity to save himself from this slow burn for a brief moment. His mind was filling up with possibilities. He excused himself, blaming it on the coffee being too strong as to not raise further suspicion, and headed towards the locker room. As he opened his locker, he began inspecting his turnout coat. What did Abe know? Had he seen something at the docks that night? He pulled out his phone only to find another new message from Xavier: Stay sharp. Things are moving faster than expected. Jack exhaled slowly. He didn't have time for Abe's suspicions, but ignoring them could be dangerous. He needed to find out exactly what he had seen—without tipping him off. *And where the hell was his lighter?* As he closed his locker, the door creaked louder than usual, as if to add extra suspense, and Jack's gaze flicked to the corner of the room, where Abe was leaning against the wall with his arms crossed.

"Something on your mind, Jack?" Abe asked, his tone light but his eyes scanning Jack the way one looks at someone when they know they are lying.

Jack forced a grin. "Just wondering how you managed to be on shift that night. Pretty impressive work, even for you."

Abe chuckled, pushing off the wall and walking past him. "Touché. I got called in to replace Carter for the evening. He was feeling unwell. Nothing like knowing someone owes you one." He gave Jack a pat on the shoulder and disappeared down the hall.

Jack stood there for a moment, the grin now slipping from his face. Abe was onto something, and Jack couldn't afford to let him dig any deeper. He would have to tread carefully—because if his best friend, who was much smarter than he claimed to be, connected the dots between the lighter, the fires, and Jack's bruises, things could unravel fast. As he grabbed his helmet and headed back toward the crew to brief them with the tasks for the day, one thought echoed in his mind: Keep your friends close. Keep Abe closer. "It is going to be a long couple of days," Jack sighed, wondering whether he could assign the least sociable task to himself or would it be easier if the earth just swallowed him whole, right at this moment.

The morning began with the usual gear checks—hoses neatly coiled, extinguishers refilled, and the engine polished until it gleamed like new. Jack normally worked alongside Abe, the two of them bantering about whose team was due for a win in their weekend basketball match. But today, Abraham was making sure he avoided him, which kind of worked in Jack's favor. By mid-morning, the team had finished a round of fire safety inspections at local businesses, jotting down notes about faulty extinguishers and blocked emergency exits. Jay grumbled about the boring corporate life some people choose, while Abe teased him for being "too delicate for the real world." Jack quietly observed the back-and-forth, his thoughts never straying far from the storm that was brewing without anyone else's knowledge. After lunch, they scrubbed the firehouse clean— mopping the kitchen floor, scrubbing the bathrooms, and rearranging the gear room. Ria told a story about her latest EMT call involving a cat stuck in a crawlspace, and by the time dinner rolled around, they were laughing so hard their sides hurt. With the sun setting, they gathered in the common room, playing a few rounds of cards while Jay lost another game of liar's dice to Ria. "Don't worry young man, you will learn one day." She would tease him the same way she teased her younger brother - with more compassion than anyone else could offer in Station #5. Jack leaned back in his chair, the calm of the evening wrapping around him like a warm blanket, and in this tiny fragment of his day, he felt an unfamiliar sense of peace. This brief moment was very quickly shattered to pieces as the firehouse alarm blared, jolting them into action. Jack's gut twisted as he heard the address—442 Redcliffe Avenue—a place that sounded oddly familiar. And just like that, the quiet day ended, and the chaos began.

***

The shrill ring of the station's alarm put the crew into motion like clockwork. Boots thudded against the floor, jackets zipped, and helmets were secured with practiced efficiency. Jack pulled on his turnout gear, the sound of the dispatch crackling in his ear: "Structure fire. 442 Redcliffe Avenue. Report of heavy flames and possible occupants trapped."

Jack's fingers faltered momentarily as he fastened the last strap of his gear. Redcliffe Avenue. The address clawed at his memory, dredging up the mental map he had drawn during countless nights of surveillance on cartel properties. His pulse quickened as a painful recognition dawned: This wasn't just another house fire. This was a key property connected to Vargas' network. The house where deals were brokered and rivals silenced. *If I didn't set a fire on that one, who did?* The fire truck roared to life as it barreled through the streets of Berkeley, sirens wailing and lights casting red and blue flashes against storefronts and alleyways. Abe sat next to him, oblivious to the storm brewing in Jack's mind, tapping the steering wheel rhythmically as he hummed a familiar tune to himself. For the first time since knowing him, Jack felt a strange and cold distance between them. Abe wouldn't even look at him, his eyes locked on the road, scanning every street corner, every passing car.

"Late-night blaze," Abe muttered. "Bet someone left a pot on the stove again." He grinned, but Jack didn't return it.

As they made their final turn onto Redcliffe Avenue, the glow of the fire lit up the night, casting flickering shadows across nearby buildings. Smoke billowed into the sky, curling like a dark hand reaching toward the stars. Flames licked at the windows, consuming the house with a ferocity that made Jack's chest tighten. But it wasn't the fire that stole his breath—it was the black SUV parked discreetly a block away, its engine idling as if waiting for something—or someone. The sleek, tinted vehicle was too familiar, too deliberate. His stomach twisted as he remembered seeing similar SUVs during his missions in Mexico, often stationed near cartel hotspots. "That's not right," Jack murmured, his voice barely audible over the roar of the engine

.

"Yeah, I mean, look at the size of this! I can almost smell the gasoline that was used to create a blaze so strong."

Jack shook his head. "I have a bad feeling about this."

"Nothing we haven't done before, Jack. Get it together." Abe jumped on the brakes until the truck screeched to a halt, which to Jack sounded like yet another desperate cry for help. They jumped out and quickly got the hose ready, their boots crunching against the pavement. A couple of nosy neighbors were poking their heads out their front doors, trying to get their eyes on some real-life action, which was often lacking in quiet suburbs like t his.

"Stay home, folks. This is not a safe place to be." Abe shouted to the bystanders.

The heat radiating from the inferno made the air shimmer like a desert mirage, but Jack and Abe moved with precision, their bodies driven by instinct and years of training. Jack adjusted the nozzle of the water hose, narrowing the stream to a focused blast as he directed it toward the heart of the blaze. Steam hissed and swirled around him as the water met fire, creating a wall of scalding vapor that clung to his skin beneath the turnout gear.

"Backdraft risk in the attic!" Jack yelled over the roar, pointing toward the upper windows, where the flames were feeding on the wooden beams like ravenous wolves. "We need to ventilate before it blows."

Abe nodded, pulling his radio from his belt. "Ria, we need ventilation on the roof! Send the rest of the crew now!"

"Roger that! The good news is - the house looks empty."

"Jack, the ceiling's starting to sag," Abe warned, pointing to the charred wooden beams overhead; the middle part now burned to a skeleton and ready to give in at any moment. "We've got maybe five minutes before it comes down."

Jack nodded, directing the hose toward the burning staircase that led to the second floor. The flames recoiled like a living creature, hissing as the water tamed them. "Let's get out before this place turns into a tomb."

As they backed out, Jack noticed movement out of the corner of his eye. One of the firefighters on the roof had cut an opening, and thick black smoke poured out like a dam that had finally burst. The ventilation was working, creating a draft that sucked the heat and smoke upward, giving the interior crew a chance to gain the upper hand.

"We've got control on the roof," Ria's voice came through the radio. "How's it looking down there?"

"Main floor's almost clear," Abe replied. "Just need to hit the last few hot spots."

Jack swung the hose one last time, extinguishing a burning sofa that had collapsed into a pile of smoldering debris.

"Let's move!" Abe shouted, giving Jack a shove toward the front door. They emerged into the night, their gear covered in soot and their faces slick with sweat. The cool night air felt like a blessing against Jack's skin, but the relief was short-lived as he turned to survey the scene.

The flames had been reduced to isolated pockets of fire, and the crew worked quickly to douse them before they could reignite. The house was a shell of its former self, its walls blackened and its windows shattered. The air was thick with the smell of wet ash and melted plastic, a scent that would cling to Jack's gear long after the fire was out. As the last of the flames were extinguished, Jack leaned against the fire truck, pulling off his helmet and running a hand through his sweat-soaked hair. His heart was still racing, but his mind was already shifting gears, replaying the events of the night and searching for anything he might have missed. Abe approached, removing his own helmet and wiping his brow with a gloved hand. "Nice work there, Captain."

Jack managed a faint smile. "Couldn't have done it without you."

Abe chuckled, but the tension between them was still there, simmering beneath the surface. "Yeah, well, don't think you're off the hook. I've still got questions."

"Great job, boys, I will meet you back at the Station!" - shouted Ria, now leaving the scene with the other brave young firefighter.

"Let's check the perimeter," Jack said, his voice steady despite the adrenaline surging through him.

Abe nodded, following him around the side of the building, where there was still thick, black smoke. As they rounded the corner, Jack's instincts screamed at him to stop. The SUV wasn't far, partially obscured by the alley's shadows, and two figures emerged from its passenger side. One was a towering man with a thick neck and arms like tree trunks, the other leaner but equally dangerous, his movements precise and calculated. Jack's hand instinctively moved toward his hip, where he kept his concealed weapon under his turnout coat. His throat tightened as the larger man drew a pistol, the gleam of the barrel catching the firelight.

"¡No te muevas!" the man barked, aiming the gun directly at Jack. Abe froze, his breath hitching audibly. "Jack—"

Jack didn't hesitate. In a split second, he ducked to the side, drew his weapon, and fired. The gunshot echoed, deafening amidst the crackling flames, which worked as a great cover. The larger man staggered backward, clutching his arm, blood seeping through his sleeve. The second man lunged toward Abe, but Jack's aim was swift and merciless. In his urgency to protect Abe, he shot two bullets, and the man crumpled to the ground, lifeless.The air reeked of gunpowder and smoke, the two scents intertwining in a way that made Jack's stomach churn, bringing back past memories he wished he could erase. He turned to Abe, who stood paralyzed, his eyes wide with disbelief.

"What *the hell* just happened?" Abe's voice was shaky, barely above a whisper.

"What the hell, Jack?!" - he was now clearly enraged, taking a few steps back as if he didn't trust Jack at all, not able to recognize the man standing in front of him.

Jack wiped the sweat from his brow, his mind racing. "I promise to explain everything, but not here and not right now. We're not safe." He glanced around, scanning the area for any sign of reinforcements. "Call the police for backup," he said, lowering his voice, "but don't mention this. If anyone finds out about the bodies, they'll write it off as cartel violence.

We can't afford the attention right now. We just say this is how we found them. Okay?"

Abe hesitated, his fingers trembling as he pulled out his radio. "Jack... what did you do?"

Jack stepped closer, his gaze steady but filled with something Abe had never seen before—desperation. "I didn't have a choice. If we didn't take them down, we'd be dead. And they know who I am. They know where I work," - Jack said through his teeth, his voice carrying a mixture of emotions.

Abe's breath hitched again. "Since when do you carry a gun? And... know how to shoot... Jack, you just killed two folks in front of my eyes, man! Tell me what the hell is going on. Are you a secret agent or something?"

"Something like that..."

"What the actual heck, Jack? Why did you lie to me for so long? I thought we were friends. I thought you were better than this."

"Look, it's not what it looks like."

Abe shook his head in disbelief and took off his helmet to wipe his forehead. He took a deep breath. His thoughts were slowly regaining more clarity as the smoke of the house fire cleared out. He thought about Jack's constant disappearances, his secrecy, and how he distanced himself. He quickly put everything together - how well-trained he was to use a gun, how he said they'd be dead if he didn't do what he'd done, the bruises on his face. He knew Jack wouldn't do anything without a reason, and he knew how righteous he was. There was only one possibility now, and he had to ask
.

"Who are you, Jack? Who are you working for?"

The words hung between them like the dark smoke they were fighting just a moment ago, thick and suffocating. Jack looked away, running a hand through his soot-streaked hair. His jaw tightened as if weighing the consequences of what he was about to say. "I'm still me, Abe. And it's not what you think," he said, his voice low but firm. "I've been working undercover for some time now. No one can know—no one. It has to stay that way. Promise me, Abraham."

Abe staggered back, his face shocked and grim, his eyes giving away his newly found clarity. "Undercover?" he repeated, almost to himself. "All those fires... the ones we responded to—were you involved in those? Did that have anything to do with your 'missions?"

"Not all of them," Jack said, his voice strained. "But some, yes."

Abe froze, his expression tightening. "What do you mean, some? What the hell are you saying? You've been burning houses when we were the ones trying to put them out? Jesus, Jack. You're supposed to be the one saving people."

Jack took a deep breath, glancing at the still-smoldering ruins behind them. "And I am. But sometimes saving people means doing things you can't put in a report. Things you can't move past, or forget. It's the line of work." He realized he justified the horrific acts the same way Xavier would, and it sent a chill down his spine.

"There are people—dangerous people—running operations that go way beyond what you'd imagine. Drug trafficking, weapons, human lives sold like products. I've been working to take them down, piece by piece." He hesitated, the weight of his words sinking in. "They cover their tracks well. If I didn't make sure certain things went up in flames, they would've gotten ahead of me. And that would've cost lives."

Abe shook his head slowly, trying to process. "So... you used our calls, our fire missions, as cover?"

Jack didn't flinch. "Not all. But when I had to, yes. It was the only way to stay close without them suspecting. You have to believe me, Abe. It wasn't just about the fires—it was about stopping something a lot worse." The distant wail of sirens grew louder, signaling that backup was on the way. Jack grabbed Abe by the shoulder. "I know this is a lot to take in. I know you're angry, and you have every right to be. But if you trust me—if you ever trusted me—you'll help me finish this."

Abe's jaw clenched, his gaze locked on the two bodies lying motionless on the ground. Finally, after a moment of hesitation that felt like an eternity, he nodded, but the fire in his eyes hadn't dimmed. "I'm in. For now. But you owe me the truth, Jack. All of it."

Jack exhaled, the tension in his chest loosening just enough to breathe. "You'll get it. Just not here."

The two men stood in the shadows of the wreckage that used to be a house, the flames of deception reflecting in their eyes as the sirens closed in. The line between right and wrong had blurred long ago, but tonight, it felt like it had been erased completely. Jack glanced at Abe one last time before turning toward the truck. "Let's go. We've got a long night ahead."

And with that, they disappeared into the chaos, their fates intertwined in ways neither of them fully understood yet.

Chapter 8

Jack parked the truck outside Aunt Meg's house, spotting Ellie sitting on the porch steps, scrolling on her phone. When she noticed him, she stood up slowly, slinging her backpack over one shoulder.

"Hey, kiddo," Jack greeted with a warm smile that genuinely reached his eyes this time.

"Hey," Ellie replied, climbing into the passenger seat.

"So," Jack said, starting the engine, "what do you say we hit up Maple's for some ice cream? You still like cookie dough, right?"

Ellie glanced at him, surprised. "You remembered?"

"Of course I did," Jack said with a grin, feeling a momentary relief from his burdens. "I told you I owed you, didn't I?"

They drove in comfortable silence for a while, the air between them lighter than it had been in weeks. As they approached Tilden Regional Park, the warm afternoon sun filtered through the leafy canopy, casting dappled shadows on the grass that danced gently with the breeze. The soft hum of distant chatter, the rhythmic carousel melody of the Merry-Go-Round, and the occasional bark of a dog blended into a peaceful symphony that should have calmed Jack's mind.

After the events from the last few days, Jack craved those precious moments of bonding with his daughter, holding on to them like they were his last, taking every detail in. She was growing up too fast. Her once chubby cheeks were now sharper, her baby fat long gone, replaced by the lean, awkward frame of a teenager on the verge of blossoming. Today, she wore her favorite purple hoodie, the one with faded stars printed along the sleeves, and had her curly hair pulled in a ponytail, which reminded him of the way Jen used to wear hers. She had been distant lately, and Jack couldn't help but wonder if it was just her age or something more.

They sat on a wooden park bench, Ellie licking her ice cream cone with so much joy. "You know, seeing you so happy makes my day," Jack said, his voice soft and sincere.

"Are you okay, dad?" Ellie asked, almost as if she wanted to cut through his thoughts and bring him back to the present moment.

Jack squeezed her hand, allowing himself a moment to just be her dad, no strings attached. "I'm better now, kiddo. Enjoying your ice cream?"

"Yeah. What were you thinking about? It's work, isn't it? You really should learn to turn off. We had a mindfulness class at school, and Mrs. Brown spoke about it."

"You mean *switch off?*"

"Yeah. Same thing." Ellie shrugged her mistake in a manner most teenagers do when they don't really want to admit they are wrong, or don't even care.

Jack sighed, leaning forward and resting his elbows on his knees. "I guess I do need to learn a thing or two about that. But right now, I was just thinking about how much I've missed this... us. And how much I've missed out on."

Ellie shifted uncomfortably, her fingers tightening around the cone. "Dad, it's fine. I'm right here, you know? You haven't missed out on anything. Besides, I know you're busy saving people. I get it. I'm just glad you're here now." Her eyes softening as she looked up at him, conveying a mix of understanding and reassurance.

I am not sure if I get it. Am I actually saving people? The people who really matter? - Jack doubted himself, feeling like every minute spent with her felt like borrowed time. Every minute that Vargas was still alive was a reason for Jack to not turn his guard down. He knew that Vargas would not let the death of his men go unanswered. If he didn't bring the cartel down soon, they'll come for him again. And if they couldn't get him, they'd come for Ellie. That was not a possibility. Jack's mind drifted to Abe, who, until recently, was the only other family he had. He hadn't heard from him since the fire at Redcliffe Avenue, and the tension between them still lingered like smoke after a blaze. Jack knew Abe was suspicious and scared—he'd seen it in his eyes, heard it in his voice. But Abe didn't know the full story, and Jack wasn't sure if telling him would make things better or worse. For what it's worth, he had to try. If something were to happen to Jack, at least Abe could be there for Ellie.

He finally broke the silence. "Me too," Jack admitted, watching her finish her ice cream. "So... how was the weekend? Aunt Meg didn't make you watch those terrible home improvement shows again, did she?"

Ellie laughed softly. "Only for a little while. But it wasn't that bad. Better than being home alone, I guess."

Jack looked at her, serious now. "You know I just worry about you, right?" Ellie shrugged. "I get it. But I can take care of myself."

Jack took a deep breath. "Maybe. But you don't always have to. I'm here too, even if it doesn't always feel like it."

Ellie hesitated, glancing down at her half-melted scoop. "It's not just that." "What is it, then?" Jack asked, lowering his voice.

Ellie looked up at him, vulnerability flickering in her eyes. "Sometimes it feels like you're somewhere else. Like your mind's always a million miles away."

Jack felt a lump form in his throat. He hadn't expected her to cut so close to the truth. "I know," he said quietly. "And I'll tell you everything. Just... not yet. But soon. I promise."

Ellie searched his face for a moment before nodding. "Okay. But you owe me another ice cream if you don't."

Jack laughed, the tension breaking. "Deal."

A breeze rustled the leaves overhead, and for a moment, they sat in silence, letting the world carry on around them. Ellie licked the last bit of ice cream from her cone and tossed the napkin into a nearby trash can. "Hey, how about we go check that Merry-Go-Round, huh? You used to love it." Jack suggested, hoping the activity will help him stay more anchored where he was, the way those golden horses were anchored to the carousel.

"Sure."

For a brief moment, the world felt normal—like he was just a dad spending time with his daughter, with nothing to hide and no danger lurking in the shadows. But the illusion was fragile, and Jack knew it couldn't last. As they stood up to leave, he glanced at his watch, a subtle reminder of the responsibilities that awaited him. "Okay, ready to go? I'll drop you off, but I need to take care of something quick right after. You don't mind, do you?" Jack asked, forcing a casual tone.

Ellie shook her head. "No, it's okay. I've got some homework anyway."

Jack gave her a smile that didn't quite reach his eyes. They drove from the park in the same comforting silence that had wrapped around them earlier, with the sunlight fading as the city's noises slowly took over the serene whispers of nature. As they neared home, the familiar sights of their neighborhood wrapped around them, a stark contrast to the secluded peace of Tilden Regional Park. As Ellie stepped out of the car and shut the door, Jack waited until he saw the light flick on and the front door close behind her. Only then did he shift the truck into gear and drive off. His smile faded as quickly as it had appeared.

The city lights blurred in Jack's rearview mirror as he drove deeper into the industrial district. The streets were emptier here—forgotten by the city, but remembered by people like Xavier. Jack's fingers drummed against the steering wheel, his mind replaying the events at Redcliffe Avenue. The gunshots. The SUV. Abe's wide-eyed stare. "What the hell did you do, Jack?" Those words echoed in his head louder than the sirens had that night. "If you ever trusted me, you'll help me finish this." But would Abe trust him again? Could he afford for Abe not to?

Jack parked his truck in a desolate lot just outside the industrial district. A single street lamp flickered overhead, casting jagged shadows against the damp pavement. The air smelled faintly of salt and oil—remnants of the docks, the place where everything had started to unravel. Xavier Graves was already there, leaning against the hood of his black SUV, arms crossed over his chest. He wore his usual dark jeans and leather jacket, his expression unreadable beneath the faint glow of his cigarette. Without glancing up, Xavier spoke: "You're late."

"I had to drop Ellie off. I wasn't bringing her anywhere near this." Jack muttered, his voice tight with a mixture of frustration and concern.

Xavier turned his head slowly, studying Jack for a beat before taking a drag from his cigarette. "Ellie? You sure it's smart to keep her close after what happened last night?"

Jack's jaw tightened. "That's why I'm here. Redcliffe wasn't just some random fire. Vargas's men were there."

Xavier's gaze sharpened, the casual tone fading as he exhaled smoke that curled up into the flickering light, a visible marker of his skepticism. "And?"

Jack stepped closer, lowering his voice. "Abe knows." The words hung heavy in the air.

"Knows what exactly?" Xavier flicked ash onto the pavement, his tone cold and measured.

"Enough." Jack ran a hand through his hair. "He saw me take them out. Two men, armed. One dead, one wounded. I had no choice."

"You killed them? In front of Abe?" Xavier's voice hardened. "And you're sure they were Vargas' men?"

"SUV with tinted windows, stationed exactly where I've seen cartel lookouts before. It wasn't a coincidence. They were going to kill us both, Xave. What choice did I have?" Jack's tone sharpened. "Abe froze. I had to act. But now... now he's asking questions. And I don't blame him, things being what they are."

Xavier cursed under his breath, pacing a few steps. "So Abe knows you're more than just some firefighter. That complicates things."

"He doesn't know everything. But he is starting to connect the dots. He isn't stupid."

"Which means if he talks, it's not just some local fallout. The wrong people in the Agency start asking questions. And this isn't exactly the kind of mission that stands up well to questions."

Jack narrowed his eyes. "Meaning?"

Xavier looked away for a moment before meeting Jack's gaze. "Meaning this whole thing—Vargas, Quinn—it's bigger than what's on paper. You know that…You think Langley signed off on deep-cover work this close to home? We're walking a line here. If the wrong division catches wind, they pull us. No explanations. No second chances. Vargas walks, and—"

"Listen, I can handle Abe. He just needs time. It's a lot to take it but he'll be fine. We'll be fine," Jack interrupted.

Xavier shot him a sharp look. "Time we don't have. You realize what this means, don't you? Vargas knows you're alive and if he knows where you work—"

"He'll come after me. Or worse—Ellie."

Silence settled between them, broken only by the distant hum of traffic and the soft crashing of waves. Xavier pulled out his phone, swiping to a news article. The dim light from the screen reflected in his eyes. "Speaking of time running out…" He held the phone out for Jack to see. "There was another protest the night you were at the docks. That's why it took so long for first responders to get to the scene. You were being set up, Jack."

Jack's stomach twisted as he snatched the phone. The article showed images of civilians clashing with riot police, fires burning in the distance. Then he saw her. Ellie. She stood in the crowd, holding a sign, her expression tense but determined. Jack's grip on the phone tightened. "She was there?"

"Yeah." Xavier's tone dropped. "Right in the middle of it. And it gets better.." Xavier swiped to another set of images, stopping on a photo that made Jack's blood run cold: Mayor Quinn, dressed in a sleek suit, shaking hands with a group of men Jack recognized instantly- Vargas's people.

Then saw the headline above: *MAYOR QUINN TO HOST CHARITY GALA HONORING CALIFORNIA FIREFIGHTERS AND LAW ENFORCEMENT—A NIGHT TO CELEBRATE LOCAL HEROES.*

Jack stared at the headline, his expression darkening. "You're kidding me."

"No joke. Quinn's pulling the perfect PR stunt. Applauding local heroes while cutting deals with Vargas behind the curtains."

Jack stepped back, processing. "So, I'm the perfect excuse. A decorated firefighter. Local hero. They'd expect me there."

Xavier nodded. "Exactly. Quinn would love to show you off. You'd blend in without raising suspicion. But listen carefully—" He fixed Jack with a cold stare. "You're there to watch, not act. Get close, gather proof of Quinn and Vargas's connection, and get out."

Jack's jaw tightened. "You're asking me to stand in a room with Vargas? Knowing what he's done?"

"I'm asking you to be smart," Xavier shot back. "You want Vargas? We need Quinn first. And this gala is our shot."

Jack glared at him, a mixture of anger and suspicion flickering in his eyes.

"Convenient, isn't it? Quinn holds a gala, honoring firefighters right when questions are being raised about all these protests. Almost like he's trying to distract the public." He took a slow step forward, lowering his voice just enough to sound casual—too casual. "Tell me something, Xave. Why didn't you take Vargas out in Los Cerros when you had the chance?"

Xavier's expression froze for a fraction of a second—just long enough for Jack to notice. The slight shift in his stance. The blink that lasted a heartbeat too long. "Are you implying I let him get away on purpose? You of all people should know exactly how much I have sacrificed for this job, Jack. To put guys like him behind bars."

Jack raised his hands slightly, stepping back, but keeping his gaze locked on Xavier. His voice softened, but his words carried weight. "Relax. I'm just asking. Seems like everything's lining up a little too perfectly, don't you think? Quinn's gala. The protests. Vargas back in the picture. Feels like someone knew exactly how this would play out."

Xavier said nothing, his jaw tightening before he looked away, flicking his cigarette into the street. Jack forced a small, almost apologetic smile, masking the doubt gnawing at him. "Hey, I get it. We've all made tough calls. I just hope you made the right one."

The tension hung heavy between them. The hum of the city seemed distant, muffled by the unspoken accusations swirling in the air. Finally, Xavier broke the silence, flicking his cigarette into the street. "Believe what you want. But if you're going to that gala, you follow my lead. No more impulsive moves. Understand?"

Jack nodded slowly, his gaze steady but unreadable. "Sure. Your lead."

But as Xavier turned away, Jack's eyes darkened. He wasn't sure who he was following anymore. "If you mess this up, it's not just you who pays." Xavier flicked his cigarette out the window and started the engine. Xavier glanced back at Jack, his tone colder than ever. "It'll be Ellie, too.. And, uh, one more thing, Jack. That cop at the docks... she didn't see your face, did she?"

Jack's breath caught. The flashing lights. The gunfire. The cold night air at the docks. Detective Sofia—he remembered her silhouette, her voice barking orders in the chaos. "No loose ends," Jack muttered. "She didn't see me. I made sure of it."

Xavier's gaze didn't waver. "You'd better be right, Jack, for both of our sakes.." Xavier warned.

Jack stood in silence as Xavier's SUV roared to life and disappeared into the night. He had been playing with fire for a long time, but now, the blaze threatened to consume everything—unless he found a way to control it. And yet, as he glanced down at his phone again—at the photo of Ellie in the protest—he knew one thing for certain - he wasn't just fighting for himself anymore.

***

The gala was the epitome of Berkeley's elite gatherings—crystal chandeliers casting soft glows on polished marble floors, waiters weaving through the room carrying trays of champagne flutes, and the hum of polite conversation punctuated by bursts of laughter. Mayor Quinn's sprawling mansion was a labyrinth of opulent rooms, gilded in luxury but laced with shadows—both metaphorical and literal. As the car stopped at the front of the lavish mansion, Jack and Abe got out, handing their keys to the valet. Jack adjusted his bow tie, the stiff fabric constricting his throat like the weight of the mission itself.

"Man, look at this place," Abe said, astounded by the size of the mansion. "My flat suddenly looks small. How could one ever afford this?"

"I'm telling you, Abe, the guy's rotten. No mayor makes enough cash to afford a place like this. Not by being a decent human being, that is." Jack's voice was low, almost lost amid the swell of a string quartet crescendo. He scanned the room, noting the careful placements of security cameras and the too-watchful eyes of certain guests.

"You know, I thought you were just hating the guy last time we spoke about this, but now I am convinced you know what you're talking about," Abe said coldly. Jack still owed him many answers to his burning questions.

As they stepped through the grand entrance, the interior of the mansion unfolded before them. The transition from the cool evening air to the warm, buzzing atmosphere of the gala was instantaneous. Around them, the gala continued in full swing, a show of wealth and power. A woman in a shimmering gown laughed a little too loudly at a joke. A businessman adjusted his cufflinks as he eyed a political rival across the room, and a young heiress flirted openly with an older senator. The chandeliers reflected in every flute of champagne, casting prismatic lights that danced across the faces of Berkeley's finest, revealing glimpses of their facades and the cracks beneath.

"Hey, look, isn't that Pat, from A Shift? Let's go say hello." Abe fixed his bow tie and rushed to see an old friend whom he shared many long and painful trainings with. His face was enthusiastic, both for the encounter and because they get to have the spotlight on them tonight - where Abe thrived.

Why did you put us in your hall of fame so suddenly, Quinn, Jack thought, skeptical about the event's legitimacy. *I wonder what you are after this time.*

The Mayor was hosting the gala under the guise of honoring California's law enforcement and firefighters for their recent efforts, especially when it came to controlling the damage from the local protest, a perfect cover for Quinn's true purpose tonight. Hidden behind the lavish decorations and champagne toasts was a secret meeting with Mateo Vargas, a man whose presence would have raised far more eyebrows if people knew who he truly was. Despite his polished appearance and the carefully crafted persona of a respected businessman, Vargas was a well-known criminal, his name whispered in connection with drug trafficking, arms deals, and cartel ties. However, no charges ever stuck—his legitimate ventures providing the perfect smokescreen.

On paper, Vargas owned and operated "Pacific Star Shipping", a successful shipping and logistics company handling cargo between California, Mexico, and various South American ports. His business had a sterling reputation, praised for fast deliveries and efficient cross-border operations, often cited as a model for international trade partnerships. But beneath the surface, Vargas used his shipping containers to smuggle narcotics, weapons, and cash across the border. His fleet of cargo ships and trucks made regular crossings between Oakland's Port Harbor and Baja California, routes that offered perfect opportunities to slip illicit goods past overworked customs officials. With a network of shell companies and false documentation, his products appeared legitimate—auto parts, electronics, textiles—all cover cargo masking the drugs and arms hidden inside. Having most of the city's best policemen and firemen contained in the mansion also opened Oakland's Port Harbour to a big shipment of drugs, one that could easily go unnoticed by the less experienced staff that was on duty. Jack's task was simple: get close enough to gather evidence of their alliance and plant a recording device in the mayor's office.

The air was perfumed with a mix of expensive colognes and the subtle fragrance of white lilies adorning each table. The grand ballroom pulsed with jazz music, but Jack couldn't hear much over the internal hum of his thoughts. As he made his way past groups of attendees, offering nods and brief handshakes, a sudden figure approached him from behind, pretending to be grabbing a champagne from a nearby server, who was skillfully holding them on a tray. It was Xavier Graves. "Stay low. Don't make a scene, Jack. We're hanging by a thread here." As Jack scanned the room for familiar faces, he spotted Mayor Quinn near the staircase, laughing too loudly as he spoke to a group of donors. The mayor's exaggerated gestures and forced charm were hard to miss. Vargas wasn't visible yet, but Jack knew he wouldn't be far behind.

He had just stepped toward the bar to get another drink when a female voice stopped him mid-step. "Well, if it isn't the man of the hour." Jack turned, masking his initial surprise with a polite smile. A woman in a sleek red dress stood before him, her dark hair cascading over one shoulder. Her eyes, sharp and curious, studied him like a puzzle she was determined to solve. "You must be Jack Singer," she said, extending her hand. "I'm Valeria Ortega, a journalist for La Jornada."

She paused for a moment, offering a polite smile. "Sorry, I didn't mean to be presumptuous. I saw a photo of your department back there—Station #5, right? You were front and center. Hard to miss."

Jack took a strong gulp and pulled himself together. His blood rushed to his head as he recognized her instantly- Detective Sofia. The woman whose life he saved down at the docks. *What the hell is she doing here? And why is she pretending to be someone else?*

"Pleasure to meet you, Miss Ortega." He accepted her handshake, masking his racing thoughts behind a charming grin. "A journalist, huh? I thought this event was for firefighters, not the press."

"I have a habit of slipping into places I'm not supposed to be," Sofia replied smoothly, her gaze never wavering. "What about you, Captain? Is this where you'd normally spend your day off?"

Jack chuckled, though the tension was building beneath the surface. "Sometimes they let us mingle with the fancy folks when they need a token hero."

"I bet," Sofia said, her tone playful, but her eyes still assessing him.

Jack shifted, loosening his bow tie slightly. "To be honest," he said, lowering his voice, "this isn't really my scene."

Sofia's smile lingered, but there was something calculating behind it. "No?" she asked. "And here I thought you'd fit right in with all these polished heroes and powerful men."

Jack smirked, deflecting. "Guess I'm more comfortable around fire than crystal chandeliers."

She leaned in just slightly. "And what brings a man like you to Mexico so often?"

Jack froze for a fraction of a second. *How much does she know?* He recovered quickly, raising an eyebrow. "Oh, I see you came prepared."

"Well, it is kind of my job." Her smile was polite, but her gaze pierced deeper.

Jack's mind raced. *She couldn't know. Surely, she must only know me as Jack, the firefighter, and it is me being paranoid. Jack, the Captain of Fire*

Station #5. Jack, whose badge was now on fire. She made him extraordinarily nervous, but he didn't flinch. He knew how to play the game, and she was about to find out. "Well, if you must know, we donate used fire equipment to the guys down there," he answered easily. "We try to help out wherever we can. Rural areas, border towns—places that don't have the resources we do, but they have ten times the fires we get here. You should know, assuming that you are from there?"

She nodded, her lips curving into a smile that didn't reach her eyes. "How noble of you. And what a brave presumption."

"Well, let's see... You are working for a Spanish newspaper, and you have a lovely foreign accent... Besides, it's rare to see a woman like you around here."

Sofia raised an eyebrow. "I will take this as a compliment."

"You should." - Jack said, questioning if he had one drink too many, or he actually meant that, since he blurted it out so effortlessly.

A brief pause hung between them before Jack tilted his head, his curiosity getting the better of him. "What about you? What's a journalist doing at a gala for firefighters? Looking for a scandal?"

Sofia's smile softened for the first time, her gaze flickering briefly away before returning to meet his. "Hardly. Though scandals do make good headlines." She took a sip of champagne, then added, "I'm working on a feature about first responders—the risks you take, the lives you save. Thought this gala might give me some... inspiration."

Jack's eyebrows lifted, intrigued but cautious. "A feature, huh? Sounds flattering."

"It's a big story." She nodded, swirling the champagne in her glass. "Especially after everything that's happened lately. The city loves a hero."

Jack narrowed his eyes slightly, but kept the smile on his face. "So this is just work for you?"

"Partly." Her expression softened. "But also... My brother was a firefighter. He loved the job. I used to tag along to these kinds of events. Not quite as fancy as this, though."

Jack tilted his head, the mention of her brother catching his attention. "So you're saying this is your scene?" He teased, offering a small grin. Sofia let out a short laugh. While he studied her for a moment, sensing there was more behind her words. "Your brother still in the field?" Jack asked, genuinely curious.

Sofia paused. The smile faded from her lips for just a moment. "No." Her voice softened. "Not anymore. He passed away a while ago. Line of duty."

Jack's expression shifted, the playful edge gone. "I'm... sorry to hear that."

Sofia lifted her gaze, offering a faint smile. "Thanks. He loved it though. Said it was the only thing that made him feel alive. I guess I come to these things because it reminds me of him."

Jack nodded slowly, studying her. *He knew what it felt like to risk everything for something bigger than yourself. Yet here he was, living a double life—pretending to be a firefighter when his real battles were fought in the shadows. Sofia's words hit harder than he expected. How many people like her brother had been caught in the crossfire of missions like his?*

"Must take a lot to still show up."

Sofia shrugged, swirling the champagne in her glass. "It does. But sometimes, you hold onto the things that remind you of the people you've lost." The vulnerability in her words hung in the air for a beat, making the moment more personal.

Jack's smile faltered for just a second. *The things you hold onto.* Her words hit closer than he expected. For a moment, his mind drifted—to Jen. Her laughter in the kitchen. The way she'd hum along to old songs on the radio. The photograph still tucked away in his wallet. The one thing he never let go of, no matter how many fires he ran into or how deep he buried himself in missions. He cleared his throat, forcing the memory back. "I get that," he said, his voice quieter now. "Sometimes, holding on is all you can do."

Sofia glanced at him then, her sharp gaze softening for a moment, as if sensing the weight behind his words. But before the moment could linger, Jack's phone buzzed. *"He is here. Back door. Stop flirting and get moving."*

Sofia glanced at his phone, her sharp eyes catching the slight change in his expression. "Looks like you've got bigger things to worry about than a nosy journalist," Sofia said, her voice soft but cutting. Meanwhile, she received similar intel through her earplug from an agent she hired to watch her back so she doesn't blow her cover.

Jack lifted his gaze to her. *Was she fishing for something?* Perhaps she knew more than she led on. But this wasn't the time to find out. "If you please excuse me... I have somewhere to be. I hope you enjoy the gala," Jack said, offering a polite nod before stepping away. Before he could slip too far, the soft clink of a glass echoed through the ballroom, followed by a sudden hush. The crowd's chatter faded as Mayor Quinn stepped forward onto the grand staircase, raising his glass with a practiced smile. His deep voice echoed through the room. "Ah," Jack muttered under his breath, stopping at the edge of the room. "Right on cue."

"Ladies and gentlemen! Thank you all for being here tonight." He paused, waiting for the polite applause to die down. "It's not every day we get to honor the true heroes of our city—our brave firefighters and law enforcement officers who risk their lives for the safety of Berkeley. Their dedication keeps our homes safe, our streets secure, and our community thriving."

The perfect cover, Jack thought, watching the mayor's exaggerated gestures and too-smooth smile.

"Let us raise a glass—to those who run toward danger when others run away," the mayor continued, lifting his champagne flute. "And let us also look ahead to brighter days for Berkeley. A city that stands tall—together."

The crowd echoed his final word with a chorus of "Hear, hear!" and lifted their glasses in unison.

"Touching speech. Almost makes you believe he's legit." Xavier's voice crackled faintly in Jack's ear, dry and sarcastic.

Jack didn't move his lips, keeping his expression neutral. "Almost." His gaze drifted, picking out familiar faces in the crowd—firefighters, police officers, politicians—but then, movement caught his eye. As the applause faded, Jack's attention sharpened. From the edge of the ballroom, a man emerged from the crowd—calm, composed, with a quiet confidence that didn't need grand entrances.

Mateo Vargas.

To most, just a successful businessman with an interest in shipping. But Jack knew better. Vargas's reputation was whispered in back rooms and police reports. He approached the mayor with a calculated smile, extending his hand. "Mayor Quinn," he greeted smoothly, "A fine speech. Truly moving."

Quinn grinned, though his eyes flickered with something colder. "Mr. Vargas. I'm glad you could make it."

They shook hands—a simple gesture to anyone else, but Jack knew what it meant. *A handshake sealing a partnership that could cripple the city.*

He looked up just in time to see Vargas and Quinn exchanging a few low words before the mayor gestured discreetly toward a corridor. Xavier's voice cut through the low hum of the gala. "That's your cue," Xavier replied, his tone shifting from casual to serious. "But be careful—Quinn's security isn't just for show tonight. Word is Vargas brought his own men too. The kind who don't ask questions."

Jack adjusted his cufflink with deliberate ease. "Good to know." As Quinn and Vargas disappeared from view, Jack moved.

"Hold up," Xavier's voice came sharp in his ear. "Two security guys just took position at the base of the stairs." Jack paused near the bar, picking up a glass of champagne he had no intention of drinking. His eyes flicked toward the staircase. The guards were exactly where Xavier said they'd be.

"Suggestions?" he murmured.

"Left side—there's a server's hallway past the restrooms. Loop around. You'll come out near the office door without being seen."

Jack smirked, setting the glass back on the bar. "Are you sure?" "Always. Try to keep up, Singer."

***

Sofia's smile faded when her eyes landed on Vargas. *Vargas? Here?* Her breath caught for a moment. Then she saw it—a cartel member brushing past Vargas, leaning in to whisper something in his ear. The man's sleeve shifted, revealing a distinct tattoo on his forearm:

A black serpent coiled tightly around a dagger.

Sofia's stomach tightened. *No... it couldn't be.* Her mind flashed back—Ensenada, the charred remains of the family home, and among the ashes, a burnt photograph. The father's arm, partially visible in the picture, bore the same tattoo. At the time, she hadn't known what it meant. Just another painful reminder of a family lost—or so she thought. But now? Now she knew. This wasn't just a random mark. It was a symbol. A connection. And Vargas was standing right next to it. "I knew it," Sofia whispered to herself, her voice tight with realization. "This is bigger than I t hought."

While the mayor continued his pleasantries, Sofia made a decision. *If Vargas is here, he's not just a guest. And if he's talking to Quinn...The mayor must be involved. I need to know how deep this goes. There have to be clues—somewhere.* Her gaze followed Vargas and Mayor Quinn as they disappeared down a corridor, speaking in low, deliberate voices. "The mayor's office," Sofia muttered under her breath. "If there's anything worth finding, it's there." Determined, she straightened her posture and began weaving through the crowd, gliding effortlessly toward the corridor. But her path was blocked. A security guard stood firmly at the door leading to the mayor's office, his arms crossed, gaze unmoving.

Think fast.

Sofia's expression softened into a confident smile. With a casual sway in her step and the poise of someone who belonged, she approached the guard. "The mayor insisted that you step aside and give us some privacy after his speech. Her tone was smooth, carrying the right mix of authority and subtle implication. The guard straightened slightly, uncertainty flickering across his face.

Sofia leaned in just enough to lower her voice. "You know how these things go. Important conversations. Private matters. I'm sure you understand." She gave a small, knowing smile and let her fingers lightly adjust the strap of her dress, the gesture just bold enough to sell the story. The guard glanced toward the corridor, hesitated for only a second, and then stepped aside without a word.

"Thank you. I will be sure to put in a good word for you." Sofia said smoothly, offering a polite nod as she slipped through the door and disappeared into the mayor's office.

The moment Sofia stepped inside, she was struck by the sheer opulence of the space. It was exactly what she expected from a man like Mayor Quinn—posh, meticulously arranged, and designed to impress. The open space was dominated by a massive vintage mahogany desk, polished to a shine. Brass handles gleamed under the warm glow of an ornate chandelier, which cast a soft light over the room. On one side of the office, a glass stand showcased a bottle of expensive whisky, flanked by two crystal glasses—untouched, but clearly for show. The whisky glinted amber in the light, a silent statement of wealth and taste. Behind the desk stretched a towering bookcase filled with old, leather-bound books. Their rusty covers looked almost identical, each spine embossed with gold lettering—titles in Latin and French, the kind of books bought for appearance, not for reading. The room was a careful balance of sophistication and ego. Every item had been chosen for effect, a message of power cloaked in culture. Floor-to-ceiling glass doors opened onto a balcony, offering a sweeping view. The doors were slightly ajar, letting in a faint breeze that stirred the heavy curtains.

All this wealth, Sofia thought, *but what secrets are hiding behind it?*

Her eyes scanned the room again. The desk had to be the starting point. *People like Quinn always kept the important things close—contracts, correspondence, the evidence I need.* Sofia moved swiftly, her fingers brushing over the polished mahogany surface before reaching for the top drawer.

Locked.

Of course. She didn't have time to pick it, not now. Glancing around, she tried the middle drawer—it slid open with a quiet creak. Inside, papers neatly stacked—invoices, charity event invitations, and letters from local business leaders. All too clean. Too perfect. Nothing useful. She rifled through them quickly, scanning letterheads and signatures. A receipt for an expensive watch. A handwritten thank-you note from a senator. *Come on, there has to be something...*

The bottom drawer was stubborn, but it gave way to reveal a leather-bound planner. business cards, and a silver pen engraved with Quinn's initials. Sofia flipped through the planner. *Meetings, fundraisers, council sessions...* But one entry caught her eye—

"Harbor—11 p.m."

The harbor? Before she could delve deeper, a faint noise froze her in place. Voices. Low. Familiar. Approaching. Vargas and Quinn. Sofia's breath hitched. *Damn, what are they doing here?!*

She shoved the planner back into the drawer, closing it silently. Her eyes darted around the room—*Nowhere to hide.* Then her gaze landed on the glass doors leading to the balcony.

Perfect.

Moments later, Vargas and Quinn entered, closing the door behind them. Sofia barely made it onto the balcony, slipping behind the curtains.

The breeze from the balcony cooled her flushed face as she pressed her back to the cold wall, ears straining to catch every sound from inside. For a moment, all she could hear was the distant hum of the city, the faint glow of the skyline stretching beyond the balcony. But then, drifting up from the ballroom below, came the sounds of the gala in full swing. The soft murmur of conversations mingled with bursts of laughter—too loud, too polished to be genuine. Glasses clinked together in celebration, the delicate chime blending with the smooth notes of jazz flowing from the band. It was a world of luxury and ease, full of small talk and hollow pleasantries—just meters away. Yet here she stood, pressed between glass and shadow, where the real power plays were unfolding. Her heartbeat slowed as she focused. The gala's noise faded into the background.

Meanwhile, just outside the office...

Jack glanced around—no one in sight. The hallway stretched empty, dimly lit by ornate wall sconces. *This is it.*

He knelt beside the doorframe, pulling out a small recording device disguised as a button. With a swift motion, he pressed it into the underside of a decorative shelf just outside the office—a spot close enough to pick up the conversation inside. He tapped it once. The red light blinked—recording live. Jack's jaw tightened. *Perfect timing.*

"Jack, they're sending someone else up. You need to move. Now." Xavier's voice was sharper now, leaving no room for argument.

"Not yet. I need more."

"You said the police wouldn't be a problem."

Jack hesitated. *Just one more minute. One more minute to hear what they're really up to.* Leaning casually against the wall, he kept his eyes on the hallway, alert for anyone who might approach. His heart pounded in his chest. Vargas's voice was cold, controlled—but there was an edge beneath the surface.

"Instead, there were more of them at the docks the other night. More, Quinn. Care to explain why?"

A pause.

"It was… a misunderstanding." The mayor's voice lacked the confidence he'd shown during his speech.

"A misunderstanding?" Vargas let out a low, humorless laugh. "That's what you're calling it? You promised me protection. Minimal attention. And yet, there they were—crawling all over the place." A sharp sound followed—perhaps Vargas placing something on the desk, or maybe just his fingers tapping against the polished wood.

"It won't happen again," Quinn said, regaining some of his composure. "I've spoken to the right people. The next shipment will pass through without incident."

"The *next* shipment?" Vargas stepped closer; Sofia could almost hear the shift of his expensive shoes on the hardwood.

Jack couldn't risk staying longer. He had what he needed—for now. The recording would capture the rest. He turned on his heel, footsteps light but hurried.

Steps echoed from the corridor, which made Quinn's head snap toward the door. "Wait—did you hear that?" The sound of a chair scraping back followed as Quinn moved toward the door, suspicion sharpening his voice. The office door flung open. With a swift step, Jack ducked behind a corner, pressing his back against the cold wall just in time. His pulse hammered in his ears.

Quinn stepped out, his eyes narrowing as he scanned the corridor. Empty.

The hallway stretched silent, bathed in dim light. The distant hum of jazz and laughter from the ballroom drifted upward, masking Jack's shallow breaths. Jack cursed under his breath.

"Damn," Xavier's voice buzzed in Jack's ear, half-laughing, half-relieved. "You like living dangerously. Thought you were done for."

"You worry too much."

"Someone's gotta." Xavier's tone softened, but carried a warning.

With one final glance at the blinking red light on the recording device, still steadily capturing every word, Jack slipped away, disappearing into the dimly lit hallway.

***

"What's wrong, Quinn? Jumping at shadows?"

Quinn lingered, peering down the corridor a moment longer.

"If you're this paranoid in your own home," Vargas continued, stepping closer to the doorway, "how do you expect to handle real problems? This isn't some petty deal we're talking about. This is the biggest operation we've run through Oakland's port in months. If the police sniff around again, it's not just your reputation on the line—it's my business. My people."

Quinn cleared his throat. "I understand. Believe me, I do. The docks are covered. No one will interfere this time. I will handle it."

A long silence stretched between them.

"They better not." Vargas's tone dropped, dangerous and final. "Because if they do, we'll have to consider... alternative arrangements."

Another pause. Then Quinn, sounding eager to change the subject: "And the next target?"

Sofia leaned in closer. Her pulse quickened.

"The warehouse," Vargas said simply. "Tomorrow night. Everything moves then. And I expect zero interference."

A pause. The room seemed to hold its breath.

"You'll have it," Quinn replied, his tone eager, almost desperate.

Vargas didn't respond right away. The silence stretched long enough for Sofia to hear the faint clink of glass—one of them pouring a drink, perhaps, or tapping fingers against the rim of a crystal tumbler. Then Vargas's voice again, softer but edged with threat:

"You'd better." Footsteps.

But this time, they didn't fade away. They were coming closer. Deliberate. Heavy. Getting louder. *They're coming out.* She couldn't risk being seen. *Not now.* Her eyes darted around the balcony - to her left, the balcony stretched further than she initially thought—long and narrow. It ran along the length of the building, connecting several rooms with tall glass doors similar to the one she had slipped through. The faint glow from the ballroom windows at the far end of the corridor offered a promise of escape. *If I can make it to the next room, I can slip back downstairs before they see me.* The door handle rattled. With careful but quick steps, she pressed herself against the wall, sliding along the balcony's edge. The railing felt cold against her fingertips. The night air bit at her skin as she reached the next set of doors.

Locked.

Her pulse hammered in her ears. The murmur of voices inside the office grew louder—Vargas and Quinn were seconds away from stepping outside. Sofia glanced ahead—one more room. *Just a little further.* Balancing her weight, she moved swiftly along the balcony's narrow path. Her heels clicked—too loud. She winced. But luck favored her. The next door had been left slightly ajar. Without hesitation, she slipped inside, easing the door closed behind her.

Inside the new room, dim light spilled from a bedside lamp. The space was quiet, empty. A guest room, opulent, but unused. Heavy curtains framed tall windows, and a plush carpet muffled her footsteps. Sofia paused, back against the door. Breath shallow. She crossed the room quickly, smoothing her dress and gathering her composure. The door to the hallway lay just ahead. With one last glance back toward the balcony, Sofia slipped into the corridor, smoothing her dress as she moved. The muffled sounds of laughter, clinking glasses, and soft jazz from the ballroom grew louder with every step.

Her pulse still raced. *The warehouse. Tomorrow night.* She had barely processed the significance of what she'd overheard—Vargas, Quinn, and the biggest operation running through Oakland's port—when the urgency to get back to the crowd took over. *Blend in. Don't draw attention.* Sofia descended the grand staircase, her heels clicking a little too fast on the marble steps. She needed time to think, to plan her next move. What was Vargas moving through the port? How deep did Quinn's involvement go? *Focus.*

As she rounded the final steps, her pace quickened- and she bumped straight into someone. Jack.

"Whoa—" Jack caught her by the arms to steady her. Sofia froze, masking her surprise behind a polite smile.

"Jack!" she said smoothly, brushing a strand of hair over her shoulder. "Sorry, didn't see you there."

Jack blinked, equally startled, though his grip loosened immediately. His smile was charming, but his eyes narrowed ever so slightly. "You're in a hurry."

Sofia stepped back, regaining her composure. "Am I?" she replied lightly, glancing down as if only just realizing her hurried pace. "Guess I didn't realize. Sorry I bumped into you like that. I could've hurt you."

Jack studied her for a beat too long. *Why is she coming from upstairs? That part of the mansion was off-limits.* His gaze flicked briefly toward the staircase, then back to her. "Didn't take you for the type to get lost," he said, his tone casual but edged with curiosity.

Sofia's smile didn't falter. "I was curious." She shrugged with practiced ease. "The mayor's house is full of surprises. Thought I'd take a look around."

She's lying. Jack knew it. *Her story was too neat. Her timing, too perfect. He had just escaped that same corridor. But why was she there?* Jack shifted his stance, glancing briefly toward the ballroom. The music played on, the same forced laughter echoing from clusters of people pretending they belonged. "You know," he said after a moment, "I am glad I bumped into you. I was just thinking about leaving and, um, I wanted to say thank you for making this night less boring."

Sofia arched an eyebrow, a small, knowing smile tugging at the corner of her lips. "Less boring? I'll try not to let that go to my head."

Jack smirked. "Didn't say it wasn't still boring—just, you know, less so."

Sofia let out a soft laugh, brushing a strand of hair over her shoulder. "Charming."

Jack hesitated for just a second before adding, his voice softer, almost sincere: "Seriously though, it's been nice talking to you." He gave a small shrug, casual but deliberate, his gaze drifting briefly toward the ballroom where the sound of jazz and distant laughter echoed. Jack hesitated for just a second before adding, his voice dropping to something softer, almost sincere: "But if I'm being honest... I could use a break from all this. I think I've had enough fancy for one night." He gestured lightly to the glittering crowd behind them—the clinking glasses, forced laughter, and the soft hum of jazz in the background. He glanced back at her with a half-smile, a spark of mischief in his eyes. "This might be a long shot, but... do you feel like getting out of here?"

Sofia raised an eyebrow, intrigued despite herself.

His grin widened. "There's a place I know—quiet, good drinks, and they make the best fries in town."

Sofia tilted her head, pretending to consider the offer, though her mind was already racing. *Best fries in town? Not quite the invitation I expected,- she thought to herself.* But this might be the perfect opportunity to get him talking. Somewhere quieter—somewhere he might let his guard down. "Best fries in town?" she repeated, a playful smirk tugging at her lips. "Jack Singer, you really know how to tempt a girl."

Jack shrugged, still watching her carefully. "No pressure. Just figured a little fresh air and something real might beat this whole... masquerade."

They held each other's gaze for a lingering moment. The music, the laughter, the clinking glasses—it all seemed to fade. Only the unspoken questions remained.

Finally, Sofia smiled, stepping just slightly closer. "Well, Captain Singer, how could I say no to fries and real conversation?"

Jack offered his arm, his smirk softening into something more genuine. "Didn't think you would." "Actually," he said, glancing back toward the grand staircase, "Would you give me a minute? I forgot to do something.

— I won't be long."

Sofia raised an eyebrow. "Let me guess, early meeting?"

Jack shrugged, flashing that same disarming grin. "Just need to say goodbye to a friend."

The staircase was quieter now. The hum of the gala faded behind him. Jack climbed with measured steps, scanning the corridor. *No sign of Quinn or Vargas. Good.* Xavier's voice crackled in his ear. "Jack. You're still in there? I thought you'd be halfway home by now."

Jack smirked faintly, touching the earpiece as he glanced around the empty corridor. "Ran into some company. Had to make sure the night wasn't a total waste."

"Company?" Xavier's tone sharpened.

"Define company."

"The journalist."

A pause.

"Ortega? She's still sniffing around?"

Jack chuckled, crouching beside the decorative shelf where the recording device blinked faintly. "She actually seems genuinely nice."

Xavier didn't skip a beat. "Jack, I don't like this. If she's asking questions, there's a chance she knows more than she's letting on. We don't even know whose side she is on. Think."

Jack retrieved the device, tucking it smoothly into his inner pocket. "Relax." His voice dropped to a lazy drawl. "I'm off the clock now, Xave. You have a good night."

"Jack—"

But Jack had already tapped his earpiece, cutting the connection with a faint smile. With the recording device secure and Xavier's warnings left hanging in the air, Jack made his way back down the staircase. Sofia waited by the door, her silhouette illuminated by the soft glow of the chandelier. He extended his arm again. "I'm sorry I kept you waiting. Shall we?"

"Lead the way."

CHAPTER 9

The night was thick with silence, the kind that felt unnatural, stretched too thin between the walls of Jack's house. He couldn't sleep again - his mind a battlefield, the remnants of the night's events replaying in his head.

But he refused to reach for the pills on his nightstand, like he usually would. He looked at Sofia, who was lying asleep next to him, her breathing steady, her body curled slightly towards him. She looked so peaceful. Jack had no idea how she could pull it off. He stared at the ceiling, feeling the weight of something unseen pressing down on his chest.

Slipping out of bed quietly, he moved to the living room - his thoughts now occupied with the night's greatest discovery that could finally put an end to his sufferings and bring justice back to Berkeley. He saw the whiskey glass from earlier still sitting on the table, untouched and now blending with the surroundings. Then he spotted his leather jacket thrown on the sofa - something he could have only done because he was distracted. He sat down next to it, and before he knew it, his fingers reached for the small recorder in its left pocket. He hesitated only for a brief second before he pressed play.

Static crackled, then voices emerged. Vargas's voice—arrogant and sharp—spoke first. "That mess at the warehouse should have been handled."

"Handled? Your boys screwed it up. Now I have loose ends to tie. I don't like loose ends, Vargas. And neither do the people above me." - Mayor Quinn was impatient, his tone demanding, but Jack could see the fear right through it.

Are you scared, Quinn? Jack thought, his face carrying a subtle smirk, his pulse pounding, eager to hear everything.

"Look, while you sit here in your fancy office and organize protests, my men and I do the dirty work. While you are still getting your payments, and I am able to supply this town's junkies with the purest drugs they have ever seen, we have a deal. But I told you - no cops messing with my business." Vargas gritted his teeth with anger.

Quinn exhaled sharply. "Yes, right, we had a deal. I let your shipments come in under the radar. I use the protests to keep the heat off you. But I don't answer for your mistakes - and especially not for drawing so much attention to you, that even my efforts can't help you."

Vargas scoffed. "Tell your man, Graves, that if this happens again, I'll be cleaning up *his* mess next." The name made Jack's blood run cold. *It can't be.* He rewinded the recording to make sure he heard it correctly, and this is not the whiskey making him delusional.

"I told you, we can't count on him. He is a tough guy to crack, only agreed to help once, and I can't convince him to do it again. You need to let him go, or we'll have more mess to deal with."

Jack bolted upright, fists clenching. *Xavier?* Before he could fully process it, a knock at the door startled him.

He turned sharply, adrenaline spiking. Another knock, louder, more insistent. "Open the door, Jack," Abe called out, his voice thick with frustration, maybe even hurt. "I'm not leaving until you do. Jack, open the door, or I will force it open!" Abe kept knocking on the front door, his thoughts blurry from all the Margaritas he drank at the party, his sole mission - to get an honest explanation from his so-called best friend. An explanation that was long overdue considering the man he trusted the most shot two men in front of him. An explanation that at least somewhat made it better for Abe - knowing that Jack drifted away from him not because he didn't like him anymore, but because he was leading a double- life. "Jack, I swear to God I won't leave until you talk to me." - before his next hit reached the white wooden door, it opened ajar.

Jack looked at Abe, his expression one of annoyance and secrecy - one that Abe by now should have gotten used to, but he knew this is not the man Jack really was underneath, and he refused to let go. "Hey man, look, Ellie's asleep and now it's not a good time..." Before he could make up another excuse, Abe interrupted and forced his way inside.

"Stop with the lies, Jack! I know that Ellie is at her Aunt Meghan's. You told me that yourself, remember? Or is there something else you are hiding? What the hell happened back there?" Abe asked, stepping inside uninvited, eyes burning with unanswered questions. "You left the gala without saying anything. You shot two men in front of me, Jack. You owe me something."

Jack ran a hand over his face, exhaustion creeping into his bones. "Ellie's not here. But I have got company. Keep your voice down."

"Wait, you went home with that journalist chick? Wow, Jack, I didn't know you had it in you..." The friend in him wanted to talk about it, but then he remembered he was mad at him, and he was there for another reason. "You know what, I don't care anymore," Abe snapped back to reality, pacing the living room. "I've known you for over a decade, Jack. You're the guy who trained me, the guy I trusted with my life. And now I find out you're... what? Some undercover government assassin? Jesus."

Jack sighed. "It's complicated."

Abe let out a dry, humorless laugh. "Yeah? No shit."

Before Jack could respond, his phone buzzed on the coffee table. A single message, burning against the screen like an ember ready to ignite into yet another wildfire into his life. *Check your front door.* A cold, twisting feeling took hold in Jack's gut. *What now?!* He moved before Abe could react, wrenching open the door. His breath hitched. A phone lay on the porch, the screen still flickering with an open video message. He picked it up slowly, his blood running cold as the image loaded.

Ellie.

His heart skipped a beat. Bound to a chair, her wide eyes filled with fear, tears running down her young, innocent face. A shadow moved behind her, and then appeared in front of the camera, eyes full of evil and cold staring at him—a gaze Jack knew painfully well. "You know what we want, Singer," Mateo Vargas drawled, his voice like oil on water. "Whatever intel you have on me and Quinn, it is not to see the light of day. Hand it over to us tonight. And maybe your daughter makes it out of this alive." The video cut off. Jack's fingers curled into a fist around the phone, rage surging through his veins, his whole world now a blazing inferno that was reflected by his face.

Abe, who had peered over his shoulder unnoticed, paled. "Oh, hell no." Jack turned to him, eyes sharp. "I need you to stay out of this."

Abe scoffed. "Not a chance in hell. We're getting her back. This is Ellie, Jack."

Jack's phone buzzed again. Another message. "Come where we met last. Don't bring company. You have two hours."

Jack was overcome by a sickening feeling. It was all too much to process, too much for him to handle alone. Ellie's life was at stake, and he had to act fast. He stormed upstairs, grabbing his gun and putting a bullet-proof vest on. He handed one to Abe, who looked at him puzzled, shook his head in disbelief, and quickly wrapped it around his chest.

Sofia, startled by all the noise, was now wide awake, still wrapped in the warm covers. "What is going on, Jack? Where are you going?"

"I have no time to explain. But I will be back. Feel free to stay here if you want.." He gave her a kiss on the forehead, knowing that his instructions won't be followed yet still playing along.

"What's the plan now?" Abe asked as they headed out of the safety of the house into the darkness before dawn, one that held many secrets and smelled like danger and fear. Vargas was always one step ahead. But Jack wasn't alone. And he wasn't about to play by Vargas's rules. There was only one man he could rely on now...

Or could he?

***

The drive to Xavier's flat was usually quick, especially in the small hours of the day when Berkeley's streets were quiet and empty. For Jack, this drive seemed like an eternity. Every second has turned into an hour, the feelings of anger now transforming into sharp focus and pure adrenaline.

"How could this happen, Jack? Do you think Meg and Pete are okay? Have you heard from them?" Abe was eager to get answers tonight, but this time, Jack was not the one holding them.

"I don't know..."

"And who the hell is this fellow? How does he know about Ellie?"

"The man you just saw is Mateo Vargas. The founder of El Sangre Cartel." "El Sangre? Doesn't that mean blood?"

"Yeah, yeah... I believe so."

"How did you even get involved with this guy in the first place?"

"Long story..."

"I have plenty of time, Jack. Question is, do you?"

"Years ago, on my first mission as a CIA in Baja, California, we went undercover to this safehouse, trying to extract information and one of our informers. It was supposed to be a quick and easy covert operation, no casualties and no men to face. I was fresh into the field, and despite my years of training, it all went sideways. The whole thing was an ambush, and the mastermind was this man - Vargas."

"Did anyone die?"

"Some of the people I went in with never got out. I will never forget how brutal Vargas was. Those people had families, they had their whole lives ahead of them... After Jen's death, I made it my life's mission to remove him from the face of the earth."

"Wow, don't you think that's a bit too much? Can't you just put him behind bars or something?"

"This man is a monster, Abraham. He is the reason why so many young kids have access to drugs around here, he treats people like they are doormats, and he has no morals. I don't want Ellie growing up in a world where she breathes the same air as him, do you? Besides, he has connections. It's not that simple "putting him behind bars." This guy can be out of there in a couple of years, and then what? Some lives are not worth saving..."

Before Abe could say anything else, they parked outside a multi-storey apartment building. Jack took the three flights of stairs to Xavier's flat like he had wings, powered by his cocktail of emotions and eagerness to save his daughter. He stormed into Xavier's apartment, his patience shattered. The door barely had time to swing open before Jack's fist connected with Xavier's jaw, sending him stumbling back into the dimly lit space.

"What the hell, Jack?!" Xavier spat, clutching his face, eyes flickering between anger and confusion, but beneath them, Jack could see all the regret he was drowning in.

"How long?" Jack hissed, advancing, his finger pointed towards him in a demanding way. "How long have you been feeding Vargas information? How long have you been playing both sides?"

Xavier wiped the blood from his lip, shaking his head. "You don't understand—"

Jack grabbed him by the collar, slamming him against the wall. "Then make me understand! You were always so strict, always so dedicated. How could you?! How long have you been feeding me lies, using me?! Ellie is in danger because of you. If you had anything to do with this, I swear—"

"They threatened my father!" Xavier choked out. "I made him hide away, so he can be safe. He was living alone in a small cabin deep in the Eastern Sierra mountains. You know how remote it is out there—isolated, no neighbors for miles. The cabin's tucked away in federal land managed by the Forest Service, surrounded by dense forests and rugged peaks. It was supposed to keep him safe, away from all of this. But Vargas found him. Said he'd gut him if I didn't step back from this one mission. I never wanted this, Jack. I swear to you. I was planning to tell you after this was all over, after we had death with him. You know me!"

Jack froze, breathing heavily and taking all the information in. Xavier's father—the only family he had left. It made sense now, the half-truths, the hesitation in Xavier's voice whenever Vargas was mentioned in their last few meetings. He released him, stepping back. "Then you better help me fix this. It seems that I have no choice but to trust you, *again.*"

Xavier nodded, rubbing his neck. "We both know Vargas won't let you walk out with Ellie alive. We need a plan."

"We don't have time for your plans," Jack said darkly. "We have to move now. This time, we are doing it my way."

"You must be Abraham." Xavier offered a handshake. "Are you sure you want to get involved in this?"

"Ellie is the closest thing to a daughter to me." Abe nodded.

"Alright, then at least gear up. If it comes to it, don't hesitate to pull the trigger. Ever used a gun before?" Xavier passed him a small handgun.

"Um, yeah, actually, I did a few years of military training before I joined the Berkeley Fire Department."

"Good. Hope you remember the gist."

With that, the three men quickly stormed out of Xavier's flat and jumped into Jack's car.

Meanwhile, there was someone watching their every single step. Sofia sat in her car, watching through binoculars as Jack and Xavier spoke. As soon as they left, she got out of bed and followed them, her instincts screaming that there was more to this than Jack had let on. And now, she had proof. Her pulse quickened when she saw Jack and Xavier rush out of the apartment, urgency written across their faces. Something was happening.

She wasn't about to sit this one out.

***

The abandoned warehouse near the docks loomed in the distance, a hulking silhouette of twisted metal and scorched walls. Its jagged rooflines were blackened by the fire Jack had set weeks ago. The charred remnants of corrugated metal still bore the scars of intense flames, twisted like the secrets the building had once concealed. Ash clung to the walls, and the faint scent of burnt timber lingered in the cold night air. As Jack approached, the crunch of broken glass and gravel beneath his feet echoed through the silent dockside. The streetlights nearby flickered uncertainly, casting long, distorted shadows. Jack remembered vividly how desperately he wanted to save Maverick's life that night, and how he had failed. Then, immediately, his thoughts went back to Ellie. "Looks like Vargas wanted to remind me of my failures," Jack muttered, eyeing the burnt-out husk. The warehouse had become a symbol of unfinished business - and tonight that had to change .

He kept low, sticking to the shadows. He could hear the faint hum of the bay's water hitting the dock, and couldn't help but wonder if Abe and Xavier managed to sneak and hide on the other side of the building unnoticed. There was no room for error - Vargas made that clear enough. The entry point Jack had used before—a side door partially melted by the fire—remained, its hinges rusted but functional. The interior was as Jack remembered: soot-stained walls, collapsed rafters, and remnants of burned crates that had once concealed smuggled goods. But now, amidst the ruins, was Ellie. She was tied to a chair, the flickering industrial light bulb overhead illuminating her frightened face.

Jack's stomach twisted. The place that had once been a battleground for another man's life was now the setting for his most personal fight yet. The warehouse was no longer just a reminder of a failed mission—it had become the final stage for Vargas's cruel game. In one quick motion, he headed towards her. All of a sudden, two of Vargas' men showed up and stopped him by cocking their guns at his head. "Not. So. Fast." Vargas appeared from the shadows, his polished shoes echoing on the rough concrete floor like a war drum. Jack's blood rushed in, his gaze fixed on Ellie. "Jack Singer. The Hero of Berkeley. May I say you have a beautiful daughter."

"Let her go. Whatever you want to do to me, do it, but she is innocent."

Vargas chuckled. "Now, now, Mr. Singer. We both know it's not that simple. I wouldn't have gone this far to meet you if it were. The recording device. Give it to me. And she walks out of here free."

"Fine, I will give you what you want. Just let her walk away from this." His heart was pounding so fast, he could hear it in his ears. He took a deep breath and reached into his pocket. He had already made a copy of the recording at Xavier's place. But Vargas doesn't need to know that. He held up the recording device. Vargas's eyes gleamed, the flames inside of them burning through Jack's heart.

"Ah, the infamous recording. See, I wouldn't have known about this if all of my men outside the office weren't mysteriously knocked out or missing. I went and checked the cameras. Clever move, Jack. But, you see, Jack, I know you. Better than you know yourself. I know you made a copy of this. You wouldn't hand it to me so easily."

The sickening feeling in Jack's stomach rushed back in. He hoped that Vargas won't suspect. Then again, he did consider it an option. *This is where I count on you, boys.* Before he could say another word, two of Vargas's men grabbed Jack. In a flash, the gun slipped from his hand and all the way across the floor. Jack fought with everything he had, managing to knock down one of the cartel members, but eventually Vargas's left hand overpowered him and brought him down to his knees, tying his hands behind his back. "You should have known better than to visit Graves's apartment," Vargas whispered, leaning close, his skin carrying the smell of tobacco and sharp perfume. "Or did you think I wouldn't notice?"

Ellie cried out as another man dragged her back, keeping her just out of Jack's reach and toying with his emotions.

"You know, Jack, I am starting to enjoy taking your precious women away from you. Like mother, like daughter..." he took a pocketknife out of his suit jacket and slowly stepped towards Ellie, with a demonic smile.

"Jen? You killed Jen? Why? Why would you do that?"

"See, Jack, I don't like it when people cross me. And you and your little friends crossed me, when you broke into the safehouse that night. Of course, I took care of most of your agents. But you... you and Graves got away. We have a saying in our cartel - *sangre por sangre*. You, Americans, would call this "an eye for an eye". See, one of you shot my dear brother-in-law that night. And he was very, very important to me."

"So you kill my wife?!"

"No, Jack, I meant to kill you."

"Jen was driving my car that day…"

"Yes, and sadly, here you are, alive and well, when she paid the price. But not for long."

Hidden outside, Xavier and Abe exchanged a tense glance. Xavier adjusted his earpiece–though they didn't have time to make a plan. He knew to pack the basics, and had been listening to everything. He planted a wire on Jack before they left, hoping it could save his life. He owed him that much. "You ready for this?" Xavier whispered.

Abe swallowed hard. "Not really, but let's do it."

They slipped through the back door. The plan was simple—cause a distraction, get Jack and Ellie out. But Vargas had anticipated them by bringing a lot more men than the usual. The warehouse echoed with gunfire as soon as Xavier stepped in, forcing them into cover.

"Damn it!" Xavier cursed. "They were waiting for us!"

"Any bright ideas?!" Abe shouted over the gunfire, taking cover.

Inside, Jack watched helplessly as Vargas aimed his gun at him.

"I'm going to end this," Vargas said, his finger tightening on the trigger. He glanced at Ellie, who was still crying, and slowly moved the gun away from Jack and onto Ellie.

"Ellie!" Jack pleaded.

Just then, an explosion shook whatever was still left of the warehouse. Smoke and debris filled the air, causing chaos and confusing Vargas's crew. "Put your gun down!" Sofia screamed, firing a shot that took down one of Vargas' men, who was standing right next to him. Vargas was shaken and took cover, ready to shoot back.

"Sofia?!"Jack gasped.

"This is our cue." said Xavier to Abe. They got out of their cover and started clearing the way down the narrow corridor so they can get to Jack and Ellie. The distraction Sofia created was enough. Xavier lunged at one of Vargas' men, disarming him. While Vargas was too busy trying to get Sofia, who was hiding in the smoke like an artist, Jack kicked his chair back in one strong motion, slamming it into the ground to break the legs. He rolled, still tied, but close enough to grab a knife from the fallen cartel member. With quick precision, he cut himself free.

"Ellie!" Jack called, diving toward her. But as he reached her, Vargas grabbed Ellie, holding a gun to her head.

"Not so fast!" Vargas growled.

The room fell silent. No one dared move.

"I said I'd kill her if you crossed me, Jack. Looks like you did. More times than I can count by now."

Jack's hands trembled, his mind searching for any way out of this. But before he could react, Abe appeared from behind, aiming for Vargas. The shot went off—but Vargas managed to shoot one back. The bullet caught Abe in the leg. He fell with a cry.

"Abe!" Jack yelled.

The chaos erupted again. Sofia fired at Vargas's men, while Xavier was pulling Abe to cover. Jack took this moment, and with all of his adrenaline surging, lunged at Vargas. They grappled like two wild cats until Jack managed to hit Vargas's gun away, which slid on the ground. Vargas reached for a knife, slashing wildly, but Jack dodged. His fist connected with Vargas's jaw—a brutal punch filled with years of rage and grief.

Vargas, bloodied and gasping, reached for his own weapon. But Jack didn't hesitate. "This is for Jen," Jack growled, lifting the gun Vargas had dropped. The shot echoed like thunder. Vargas collapsed, lifeless.

Silence. The fight was over.

Jack turned, breathless, to see Sofia holding Ellie in an embrace, covering her eyes to make sure she wouldn't see any more of this. "It's over," he said, pulling Ellie into his arms. "It's finally over." He sighed out with the sense of relief that he hadn't felt for years. But his relief was short-lived.

"Abraham, stay with me!" Xavier was down on the ground, next to Abe's collapsed body.

"He is losing a lot of blood."

"We need to get him to a hospital—*now!*" Sofia shouted.

Together, they carried Abe out of the burning wreck of the warehouse. Vargas's remaining men were either dead or running, the empire he built crumbling with him. As they sped through the streets, sirens in the distance, Jack held Ellie close. He looked at Abe, who barely clung to consciousness. "Stay with me, man," Jack whispered. "You're not going out like this." For the first time in a long while, Jack felt the weight lift—Vargas was gone. But as he glanced at Sofia and Xavier, he knew there were still questions. Loose ends.

But that was for another day. For now, they had survived. He gets to bring his daughter home. And that had to be enough.

EPILOGUE

The morning sun filtered through the wide windows of a small diner nestled on the corner of 4th Street. The smell of fresh coffee and sizzling bacon lingered in the air. Jack Singer sat in a worn booth by the window, the same booth he and Jen used to share for breakfast on lazy Sundays. The memories were softer now, no longer sharp with grief. With Vargas gone, the air felt crisp; the sun shined brighter. Justice had been restored, and for the first time in years, Jack felt he could breathe. Across from him sat Xavier Graves, his ever-serious expression softened by the steam rising from his coffee cup. The two men sat in comfortable silence for a while, watching the world pass by outside. "So," Jack finally said, stirring his coffee, "I hope you know that this is it for me. I'm done."

Xavier looked up, his brow lifting slightly. "Done?"

"Yeah." Jack leaned back in his seat, a small smile tugging at his lips. "As much as I would miss your grim face, I am done living a double life. Ellie needs me, and I want to be there for her. I want peace. Balance. I think I've earned that."

Xavier took a long sip of his coffee, nodding. "You have." He set the cup down and met Jack's gaze. "I owe you an apology, Jack. For everything. For betraying your trust. For dragging you into all of this."

Jack shook his head. "You did what you had to do. I get it. Your father's alive because of it. And Vargas... he is gone. That's what matters."

A shadow crossed Xavier's face, but he gave a curt nod. "My father's well. He's moving back to the city. Wants to be closer, you know? After all those years up in the Sierras, he says he's had enough of living like a lone wolf."

Jack smiled, glancing out the window. "That's good. He deserves that." They fell silent again. Xavier tapped his fingers against the ceramic mug. "I got promoted, you know. After we caught Vargas. More boring desk work. Better pay. Fewer field ops—if any."

Jack laughed, a genuine and pure sound that filled the small space. It sent Xavier years back, when he first met Jack, and he had this innocence and pure joy in him. "Sounds like a good thing for you."

Xavier gave a noncommittal shrug. "Maybe. I'm not sure. The field's all I've ever known."

Jack looked at him, studying the man who had once been his mentor, his betrayer, and now, somehow, his friend again. "Maybe it's time to know something else. We both deserve that. Though I am not sure how I will make peace with a normal, boring life, you know?"

Xavier looked back at him, and for the first time in years, there was no tension between them. Only understanding. "You're right," Xavier said, chuckling. "We deserve boring." As they stood in silence for a brief moment, they noticed another news report on TV, and Jack couldn't help but stare at Quinn's face with fire in his eyes. "Oh, yeah. Quinn, the mayor. Sorry, it's a little bit more complicated. He's untouchable...for now. At least we caught the bigger fish."

"Yeah, I guess so..." They finished their coffee in silence, the weight of the past lifting, leaving room for something new. Jack glanced at his watch. "Ellie will be waiting. Time to head home."

Xavier stood, pulling on his coat. "Tell her I said hello."

"I will." As they stepped outside, the morning sun warming their backs, Jack turned to Xavier. "Hey. Let's not wait too long for the next brunch. Don't be a stranger just because you got your cool new promotion, alright?"

Xavier gave a rare smile. "We won't."

Jack watched him walk away, blending into the crowd. He took a deep breath, turning towards home. For the first time in a long time, he felt the weight lift. Vargas was gone. Ellie was safe. The fight was over.

And maybe, just maybe, peace was finally his.

***

Meanwhile, miles away, another kind of fresh start was taking shape, one that involved a shift not just in place but in purpose.

Detective Sofia Calderón stood at the window of her office in the bustling heart of San Francisco. The cityscape spread out before her was a far cry from the dusty streets and simmering tensions of her old life. The office bore the insignia of the DEA, a badge she now wore with a mixture of pride and anticipation. Today marked not just another day at her new job, but the first day of the rest of her life.

Leaving her past behind had not been an easy decision. But as she tidied her belongings in her new office, methodically placing each item with thoughtful consideration—a sign of her fresh start—Sofia felt ready to leave the shadows of her old life behind, feeling the weight of her past decisions lifting like a shroud from her shoulders. As she looked through her things, her eyes settled on a framed photo on her desk—a photograph of her and her brother, taken just a year before his untimely death. "For Álvaro," she whispered, her voice a mix of resolve and hope. He had always believed she was meant for bigger things, and though he was gone, his faith in her remained a guiding force.

The battle against the cartels would be long and fraught. But now, she was exactly where she needed to be.

***

Abe lay in his hospital bed, the steady beeping of the monitor a comforting reminder of his steady recovery. The room's door swung open, and Ellie, with the uncontained enthusiasm of youth, dashed toward him, her arms outstretched. "Not so tight, Ellie!" Abe exclaimed with a pained chuckle as she hugged him, perhaps a little too eagerly for his current state.

"Sorry, Uncle Abe," Ellie said, pulling back with a sheepish grin.

He looked over her head at Jack, who stood by the door, a soft smile on his face. "She's getting stronger. Are you sure you can handle her?" Abe teased.

Jack walked over, his concern momentarily overshadowed by the warmth of the scene. "How do you feel?" he asked, turning his attention back to his friend.

"Better now that my backup has arrived," Abe replied, his eyes twinkling as he glanced at Ellie.

The room filled with their laughter, echoing off the sterile walls and filling the space with warmth. Jack sat on the edge of the bed, his expression turning thoughtful. "Once you're out of here, we should take that fishing trip we talked about," he suggested, the idea hanging in the air like a promise to return to normalcy.

"Sounds perfect," Abraham agreed, his gaze shifting to Ellie. "And maybe teach this one how to not scare away the fish."

Ellie rolled her eyes, but her smile was bright. "Deal, but only if we get ice cream after."

It was these moments, fleeting and filled with laughter, that reminded them that no matter the challenges ahead, they had each other.

***

But far from the sunny streets of Berkeley, in a dimly lit room cluttered with faded photographs, guns and thick with smoke, a figure stood before a cork board. A photo of Jack Singer was pinned at its center. The figure's face was obscured in shadow, but the hand was steady—gripping a knife. With a slow, deliberate motion, the blade pierced the photo; the tip embedding deep into the wood behind it.

The figure stepped back, eyes cold with resolve. Mateo Vargas's closest nephew had learned of his death. The message was clear: Jack Singer's story wasn't over. Not yet.